SENT TO HIS ACCOUNT

SENT
TO HIS
ACCOUNT

EILÍS DILLON

PERENNIAL LIBRARY

Harper & Row, Publishers, New York
Cambridge, Philadelphia, San Francisco, Washington
London, Mexico City, São Paulo, Singapore, Sydney

A hardcover edition of this book was originally published in Great
Britain in 1954 by Faber and Faber. It is here reprinted by arrangement with Eilís Dillon.

This work was originally published in Great Britain and is fully
protected by copyright under the terms of the International
Copyright Union.

First PERENNIAL LIBRARY edition published 1986.

Library of Congress Cataloging-in-Publication Data

Dillon, Eilís, 1920–
  Sent to his account.

  "Perennial library."
  I. Title.
PR6054.I42S46 1986   823'.914   85-45631
ISBN 0-06-080805-5 (pbk.)

86 87 88 89 90 OPM 10 9 8 7 6 5 4 3 2 1

SENT TO HIS ACCOUNT

1

Miles had just finished making up Mrs. Henley's egg book when his landlady rapped at the door.

"You are wanted on the telephone, Mr. de Cogan," she said, "and may I add, not for the first time, that it is no part of my business to climb the stairs with trivial messages for my guests. If you wish to have a private telephone number, no doubt the Post Office——"

He let her run on to the end of her piece, and then said kindly:

"Thank you, Mrs. Doran. Tell whoever-it-is that I'll be down in two shakes."

As usual, she softened enough to show her big yellow teeth in a grin. Bowing politely, Miles shuddered as he held the door for her. An insult to her sex, he reflected, as she pattered downstairs. That's what she was.

He followed more slowly a moment later. He had put on a bit of weight lately, on account of all this sitting down. It was bound to show in the end. Still, to be as healthy as he was at fifty—that was something to be thankful for. And his hair being snow-white seemed to inspire confidence in his various employers. Perhaps after all a little rotundity was just what he needed.

He reached the telephone in the hall, handily placed on the table near the kitchen door so that Mrs. Doran could hear at least one side of the conversation. Miles heard her excited breathing behind the panels as he put the receiver to his ear. He fixed a non-committal eye on the coy red lantern that shaded the electric light, and in a completely dead voice, killed by long practice, said:

"Yes . . . yes. . . . Indeed. . . . . Certainly. . . . I shall be very pleased. . . . Oh, yes, undoubtedly. . . . Thank *you*. . . . Good-bye."

Then he hung up. A gratifying snort reached him from the other side of the door. He grinned fiendishly to himself, as he always did when he had succeeded in foiling her. He was half-way up the stairs to his room when he stopped and clutched the banister with a groping hand. The impact of the conversation he had just had was like to send him headlong down the stairs again. He had been so pleased at having scored over Mrs. Doran. Slowly he dragged himself up the rest of the way and along the corridor to his room. He fumbled with the handle and went in, closing the door carefully behind him so that the old harpy below would not guess that something out of the way had happened. Suddenly he pirouetted across the room, and landed sitting on his bed, waving his arms, longing to emit a yell of joy, but restrained by some inborn element of caution. The old harpy did not matter any more! Nothing mattered! Hallelujah! In future his bed should be of ivory, of beaten gold his throne! Hallelujah!

The voice on the telephone had said:

"Is that Mr. de Cogan? . . . Mr. Miles de Cogan? . . . We have been looking for you for weeks. Your cousin, Sir Miles de Cogan, of Dangan House, Dangan, Co. Wicklow, has made you his heir. He died five weeks ago, but we were not able to find you. Can you come into the office this morning, so that we can discuss it? . . . About twelve o'clock? . . . You *are* Miles de Cogan, aren't you? . . . Thank you. . . . Good-bye."

Miles's eye lighted on Mrs. Henley's egg book. He darted across and picked it up, thinking perhaps to rend it with his teeth. But then he paused. Caution before all. He might need her again. He laid the little book down and went across to look out of the window at Mrs. Doran's cat on the garden wall. Strange how it had a sort of family resemblance to Mrs. Doran. Must be the mange. The solicitor had not said what his cousin,

Sir Miles, had left him. A mortgage and a few debts, possibly, or perhaps a few little responsibilities to be educated in the path of virtue. He knew nothing about Sir Miles, though he had always known of his existence. Had there been a little something, he wondered? A flat in Paris, or Vienna, or London, or in some other similar painted port of sin? One could not have such luxuries without money, but once one had had them, there might be no more money left. That Miles knew from his experience of accounting, such as it was. And it all went to show how mud sticks, he thought severely. It must have been forty years since he had overheard his father cast veiled doubts on the morality of his titled cousin.

He stuck his head out of the window and saw that a bus was coming up from Donnybrook. His watch was broken, and he had not been able to afford to have it mended, but he had become quite accomplished at telling the time by other means. The sun having reached the hole in the linoleum by the washstand, he knew that it was half-past eleven. Half a minute later he was standing on the footpath, brushed and smooth, leaning on his silver-banded walking-stick, waiting for the bus.

It was far too early when he reached St. Stephen's Green, where the solicitor's office was. He walked into the Green among the flowers, to pass the time and calm his excitement. He even stole a rose-bud for his buttonhole when no one was looking. It was good enough for that rose-bud, he thought, as he admired its pert little face nestling against his lapel. It had no business to flower in the middle of May. The air was like wine—vin rosé, drunk in a Paris café, to be precise. The traffic hummed a Strauss waltz in the distance. Miles's heart bounded within him quite alarmingly.

At last all the clocks began to strike twelve, tenors, basses, bass-baritones and one or two drawing-room sopranos. When they had finished, decency made him wait for another minute or two before crossing the street to the office. He had marked it well in advance. He fluttered up the steps on airy wings, but in the front office was a clerk who might have been a litter sister of Mrs. Doran. She brought him down to earth with a curt:

"Well?"

He said that he had an appointment with Mr. Barne.

"You're late," she snapped. "I'll find out if he can see you."

As she passed through the door marked "Private" in letters of gold, Miles thought how satisfying it would be to hit her an almighty wallop with his walking-stick. But he always suppressed impulses like that, so he leaned firmly on his stick, while he examined an engraving called "His Only Pair", which hung on the wall between a builder's calendar and a menacing steel filing-cabinet. The picture represented an industrious mother mending a pair of trousers for a depressed small boy, who sat in his shirt-tails on a table looking on. Other members of the family, who all appeared to be shattered by the impropriety of the business, sat or stood about with hang-dog expressions. Miles whistled derisively through his teeth at them.

Now the door marked "Private" opened, and he was bowed into the inner office, this time with apologies and obsequious smiles, by the clerk. But he forgot her at once, and turned his full attention to the man behind the desk.

Miles rather liked Mr. Barne. He was small, and he looked meek, and somehow lopsided. But from time to time he revealed by a remark that he had an agile little soul springing about inside him. He examined Miles from head to foot with an interest which he made no attempt to conceal. At last he said:

"Not much family resemblance."

"Indeed?" Miles raised his bushy white eyebrows in surprise. "We pride ourselves on our family likenesses. The de Cogans have an insatiable family pride."

"I am well aware of that," said Mr. Barne in a depressed tone. "I acted as agent for your cousin almost all my life."

"Tell me about him," said Miles. "I barely knew of his existence. I never met him. What did he look like?"

Mr. Barne opened a folder on his desk.

"As it happens I have a photograph of him here. It is an enlargement of a passport photograph, and a bit blurred, but you may take it that he looked like that."

Miles studied his cousin's portrait with deep interest. It showed a very small, thin head, and drooping shoulders. There was a drooping moustache, too, a rabbit-toothed, weak grin, melancholy eyes and a goatee beard clinging perilously in space. Miles remarked that he was glad there was no family resemblance to speak of. Mr. Barne gave a quick, appreciative smile. Miles put his next question cautiously.

"What way did he live? What sort of life did he lead?"

"Quiet, mostly," said Mr. Barne. "He was not married, as you probably know, and his sister kept house for him until a couple of years ago. It used to worry him that he had no heir, but when I suggested that he get married, he did not seem at all taken with the idea. It took him a long time to decide about his will. You see, he hated Catholics," said Mr. Barne apologetically. "He thought they were never quite gentlemen."

Miles chuckled.

"He should read Evelyn Waugh," he murmured. "His Catholics are appallingly exclusive fellows. Some of them will hardly speak to a priest. It makes my soul expand to read him. By the way—I hope you won't mind my asking—what persuasion are you?"

"Well, you see, Mrs. Barne is Church of Ireland, so I suppose I am too. It was a pity Sir Miles never met you, Mr. de Cogan. That would have set his fears at rest."

The most delicate compliment of my life, thought Miles, delighted.

"As you mentioned family pride," Mr. Barne went on, "you will understand that Sir Miles could not bear to leave Dangan to anyone but a de Cogan. We went to great lengths to find—an heir to his liking." He grinned triumphantly. "But at last we had to admit ourselves defeated. Sir Miles knew your father, and that there was a son called Miles. He was sufficiently

11

pleased at the Christian name to forgive the religion. At first he wanted to put all kinds of conditions into the will, but I persuaded him not to. I told him that he would end by having no heir at all, and that the Government might even get possession eventually. He hated that prospect so much that he gave in. He had all the papers ready for probate so that his heir could step in at once."

"What were the conditions?" Miles asked curiously.

"You were to have been in the British Army or Navy in your youth, for one thing, and you were to marry and have a son within a specified time. Yes, I know," said Mr. Barne hurriedly, at Miles's grin. "We often find people wanting to play God from beyond the grave."

"Those conditions would have finished me," said Miles.

"I stopped it all, at any rate," said Mr. Barne, "and the estate is yours unconditionally."

"How much?"

"I beg your pardon? Oh, yes, yes." He fumbled among his papers again. "Ah, yes, here we are. First, there is Dangan House—a fine place. I've stayed there from time to time. Not much land—less than two hundred acres." Miles had once tried to have a window-box, but Mrs. Doran had put a stop to it. "Then there is the village of Dangan. Most of that will be yours. Ground rents, houses, a little flour mill and so on. And about forty thousand pounds in the bank," he finished abruptly and dropped the paper on the desk.

Miles made no comment for a moment. Then he said:

"In the bank? What an odd place for forty thousand pounds."

"It was the subject of many arguments, Mr. de Cogan," said the solicitor. "I wanted him to put it into shares of one kind or another, but he would not touch any of it. He said that the bank was the place for money, and there it stayed. I'm sure you will be more open-minded than he was."

"Oh, yes. It's a shame not to put money to work," said Miles, who had fifteen pounds' worth of brewery shares, out of the dividend of which he had been accustomed to buy himself a splendid new tie every Christmas.

"Did Sir Miles make provision for his sister?" he asked now. "Is she married? Has she money of her own? And what is her name?"

Only by the speed of his questions might he have revealed his excitement. Mr. Barne looked at him sharply, and answered the questions.

"Her name is Germaine," he said. "I knew her well, of course, while she lived at the house. A couple of years ago, Sir Miles had one of the front lodges put into order for her, and she went to live there alone. She has an income of her own, but I think it is not much. I don't handle her affairs at all. Sir Miles left her nothing in his will."

"Nothing at all?"

"Nothing, and he even made a point of saying that he had repaid her in plenty while she acted as his housekeeper, and that she had had enough out of him—so that she would not be able to contest the will."

"What sort of lady is Germaine?"

"A real old maid. I have no use for her," said Mr. Barne. "She has one or two friends in the village. I tried to stop Sir Miles, but it was no use. I told him there would be no satisfaction in insulting his sister after his death, but he said it would give him great satisfaction to think of it beforehand, and that in any case he intended to haunt Dangan House and the lodge, after his death."

"And does he?"

"I have had no complaints," said Mr. Barne primly.

"I wonder why he hated his sister so much. Do you know why they quarrelled? I suppose that it was after a quarrel that she left the house?"

"I'm afraid I know nothing of that," said Mr. Barne.

"I should very much like to know it," said Miles. "What age was he when he died?"

"About seventy. He had been nursing a bad heart for twenty years. His sister is a good deal younger, not yet sixty, in fact."

"I wish I had known him," said Miles wistfully. "It might help me to understand my own position."

Mr. Barne coughed, not wishing to disagree. Then he said:

"How soon would you like to go down and see the place?"

Miles longed to shout:

"At once!"

But above all he wished to preserve the decencies, so he said airily:

"Whenever you like. I'll be interested to see it all."

"Naturally." Mr. Barne thought, with a hard little wrinkle between the eyebrows. "I could manage to-morrow—that is, if you would like me to come," he added hastily.

"I should be delighted," said Miles, and he meant it.

He had not at all liked the prospect of arriving alone, and perhaps unwelcome.

"There are cars at Dangan, but that is no use to you," said Mr. Barne. "We could drive down in mine. I will telephone Mrs. Hooper and say that we shall be there for lunch."

"Who is Mrs. Hooper?"

"The housekeeper. A very good person. There is never any trouble about staff at Dangan. We can look over the place in the afternoon, and I can drive back after dinner."

"Would you like—could you please spend the night?" said Miles. "I should appreciate it very much if you would." Mr. Barne looked surprised. "Just in case Sir Miles does haunt the place," he pleaded.

Mr. Barne laughed.

"Very well. I often stayed the night on former occasions. Sir Miles liked to discuss business after dinner." He fumbled among the papers again, and looked embarrassed. "You won't mind my asking—are you in need of money now? I mean, I can advance you some, if you wish."

"Plenty of time for that," said Miles heartily. "We can talk it all over to-morrow."

"You might let me have some evidence of identity," said Mr. Barne as he stood up. He grinned, showing a great many teeth. "It's purely formal now. I have been finding out all about you. By the way, I should mention that you inherit the baronetcy, too."

"I suppose that can't be helped," said Miles. "I certainly won't be in a hurry to assume it."

"No hurry," said Mr. Barne.

He led Miles out through a second door into the narrow hall. As he crossed the office, Miles said curiously:

"I have been looking at that extraordinary picture since I came in. Do you like it?"

He paused before the picture and availed himself of the opportunity to peer more closely at it. It hung at one side of the door and from a little distance it looked like a human skull in black and white. On closer inspection, however, it proved to be a lady dressed in the fashion of the late nineteenth century, seated sideways at a dressing-table, examining her reflection in the glass. Underneath was a caption: "Vanity of vanities." Miles thought it quite disgusting. Mr. Barne sensed this and said apologetically:

"My wife put it there. She said it was to keep my mind on higher things. I can't say that it does. I'm afraid my eye has learned to slide around it—you know how that happens."

Miles began to wonder about Mrs. Barne. He made no comment, however, though he would have liked to recommend that the picture be turned with its face to the wall. On the doorstep he remembered to arrange for Mr. Barne to call with the car at Mrs. Doran's in the morning. Then he shook hands carefully, and walked off trying to look unconcerned. He went into St. Stephen's Green again, and wandered about.

"Dangan House and two hundred acres," he said to the ducks on the pond.

15

"Houses, ground rents, a mill in the village," he remarked to the tulips.

"Forty thousand pounds in the bank," he said earnestly to an astonished dog wandering illegally off its lead.

He twirled his walking-stick, and controlled an impulse to skip and run along the path. Then he muttered lugubriously:

"Vanity of vanities. Oh, hang Mrs. Barne!"

And he left the Green and started off briskly for Grafton Street.

2

The next few hours were unashamedly happy. A nagging, cynical voice within tried to spoil his fun by reminding him of his often-expressed principles concerning ownership and the dead weight of property. He could not yet feel that his property was a dead weight. He dismissed all philosophy in the simple pleasure of buying a new suit of clerical grey, in keeping with his years and chosen carefully. He also bought an overcoat, socks, shoes and gloves and all the other appurtenances of a gentleman. He was amused to observe how the manager of the shop was content to clothe him completely, although he had never seen him before, and to accept his new address at Dangan as security for his bill.

"It must be that I look a Real Princess," he said to himself, remembering Mr. Barne's compliment with undiminished pleasure.

He lunched at the Shelbourne Hotel among his peers, recklessly spending his pocketful of silver. He deeply enjoyed the company of the aged colonels who sat about him, remarking: "Gad, sir!" and the thin, oddly-dressed ladies who hardly spoke at all. This was the life, without a doubt. He loved the supercilious waiter, and the grand gloom of the lounge. It was incredible and marvellous, but it was all his.

Afterwards he went to his bank and withdrew his thirty-one pounds, which he had intended to spend on a holiday in Paris. As the clerk carelessly handed him the money, Miles thought of the three years' labour that had been necessary to save it— his watch unmended, his shoes worn until the pavement tickled the soles of his feet, his hair grown too long, his razors used

17

until they were unfit to pare pencils—these and many more ignominious economies he had practised. He was glad now that he had been so strong-minded, though the money would be put to a very different use from the one of which he had dreamed.

Outside the bank he took a bus to Canning Street, where all his employers had their shops. He alighted outside Mrs. Henley's shop. Her daughter, Maggie, was at the door, counting cabbages into a box.

"Good afternoon, Miss Henley," he greeted her, and she blushed with pleasure.

It was half-past four now, and the shop was full. He picked his way between racks of vegetables and crates of eggs, around pyramids of groceries and banks of pigs' heads, to the back of the shop. Mrs. Henley saw him and called out cheerfully:

"Hold on there, Mr. Cogan! I'll be with you in a moment."

He held on. She always called him Mr. Cogan, but he noticed that he did not resent it now. In fact, it sounded friendly, almost nostalgic. Mrs. Henley was immensely fat, dressed in a print overall with the sleeves rolled up to leave her monumental forearms free. Her fingers were agile sausages, dancing in a cheerful ballet over the counter, catching and wrapping and flipping parcels so fast that it was quite painful to watch them. She seemed to have no respect for the goods she handled, Miles always thought, as if she knew exactly what they were up to, and intended to put a stop to it. She was a good business woman, and she paid Miles ten shillings a week to make up the accounts for which she had no time herself.

It was ten minutes before she came towards him, at a sort of ambling run. She pushed open a door at the back of the shop and preceded him into a dark little parlour. The dim light came through a heavily curtained window that peered out on to a dank, green-flagged yard. The table, the chairs, the mantel-shelf and the nasty little draped sideboard were all covered with account-books. Mrs. Henley said, as she always did:

18

"I can't ask you to sit down, because there is no place to sit."

Then she stood expectantly poised, ready to run back to her shop the moment he had finished with her.

"Is it the egg-book?" she prompted him, for he hardly knew how to embark on his incredible tale. "Did that one add in a few dozen again, the old hairpin? I suppose she thought she could cod me, the creature, sure 'tis hard to blame her, and she not knowing the clever man she has to deal with."

Again she looked at him expectantly, so that he had to begin:

"I have finished the egg-book, and, strangely enough, it was quite correct."

"Strangely enough is right," said Mrs. Henley. "That's the first time in history. I wonder what came over her? Is that what you came to tell me?"

"Well, no," said Miles modestly. "I just wanted to say that I am about to give up the work."

"Arah, don't do that at all, Mr. Cogan! Sure, what would I do without you? Is it more money you're wanting? I could make it a pound a week, if you like, and maybe if I asked them all the other ladies would do the same——"

"No, no! It's not that at all." In his embarrassment, Miles hardly spared a thought for what that extra ten shillings would have meant to him yesterday. "It's just that I have been left some property, and I won't have to work any more."

Mrs. Henley grasped his hand and shook it vigorously.

"Well, now, isn't that grand? Man, dear, I never heard better news in my life! But tell me now, don't you think you might be bored, like, with no work to do? Couldn't you keep up the little bit of work, for the interest of it, like?"

Miles explained kindly that he hoped to have other pursuits, enough to keep him busy. He did not add that he hated figures with a deadly and personal hatred, and that he hoped that he would never again be condemned to spend his days bent over their crooked, malignant little faces. At last she accepted his resignation, and Miles went on to suggest that they have a party to celebrate.

"I'd like to ask the others, too," he said. "And it will have to be to-night, because I'm going away to-morrow morning."

Mrs. Henley interposed firmly:

"Just leave all that to me. I'll send Maggie around to them all." She stopped suddenly. "Where will we have it?"

"Not at my place," said Miles. "Mrs. Doran would never allow it."

"True for you. You're not going to ask *her*, are you?"

"I had thought of it," said Miles, "but I doubt if she would enjoy herself."

He could imagine her looking down her long yellow nose at his aproned friends.

So they arranged to have the party in Mrs. Henley's upstairs parlour, which was big enough. Miles gave her the thirty-one pounds to buy provisions, and a small present for each lady. Then he went out through the shop again, having promised to come back at eight o'clock sharp. On the doorstep, Mrs. Henley gripped his arm.

"What about the husbands?" she asked. "Will we have them, too?"

"I thought there weren't any—I mean——"

"There are indeed, six of them. Mrs. O'Brien and Mrs. Mulligan is widows. But there's five along with my own man. Sure, we may as well let them come, the creatures. They won't do any harm, and they'll be useful for opening the bottles."

So Miles agreed, and came out into Canning Street again, on the edge of hysteria from inward laughter. How wonderful to be married to a Mrs. Henley, he thought. Complete security, everlasting chat, no work—it was a prospect of paradise. He wondered what Mrs. Mulligan and Mrs. O'Brien had done to their husbands. Overlaid them, he supposed.

At home an hour later, he gently told Mrs. Doran that he

would be leaving in the morning. To his astonishment, her eyes filled with tears.

"After all those years, Mr. de Cogan, you're like one of my own," she said. "And I was only saying last evening to Mrs. Cross that I expected to have your wake in the parlour! Always such a gentleman, I said to her, never banging the doors or bringing in noisy visitors. I'm going to miss you a great deal, Mr. de Cogan."

And she ran into the kitchen, to hide her tears. Who would have known, thought Miles, that such devotion lay concealed behind her snarling bark and twitching, curious ears. It would be nice not to see her again. He wondered at himself for having lived in her house all these years, when he might have enjoyed the rumbustious flavour of Canning Street.

The party was a great success, and Miles enjoyed every moment of it. He arrived at the door at five minutes past eight, and was swept upstairs at once to the big room where everyone was already assembled. First there was a huge supper of grinning pigs' heads and cabbage and potatoes. Afterwards they sat about companionably chawing pigs' feet and drinking stout and port, while they all congratulated Miles on his good luck. The six little husbands were there, waiting on their magnificent wives, opening stout bottles, carving, handing vegetables, speaking to each other in subdued voices. For all that, they had an independent air, and they paused now and then to take a quick drink or a bite of food. Their wives spoke to them with unfailing courtesy. The women talked shop among themselves, for they were all in the grocery business. Later there was tea and cakes and more stout, and then Mrs. Henley handed out the presents which she had carefully selected according to her knowledge of each lady. Miles was astonished that she had had time for it all.

"It was easy enough," she said airily. "The shop was full of customers when you left, and I just shut the outside door, and there I had them all! They came up and cooked the grub while

21

I went out and did the shopping. The pigs' heads and the spuds and cabbage came out of the shop, so there was no delay."

Presently they began to sing, all together at first, and when their shyness had worn off there were a few solos. Mrs. Murphy, in a peculiarly sweet voice, sang "Down by the Sally Gardens", and Mrs. Roche and Mrs. Byrne followed more raucously with "Home, Sweet Home" and "The Garden where the Praties Grow". Then the smallest husband, Mr. Byrne, sang very fiercely "The First Cork Brigade". It was one o'clock when the party broke up.

On Mrs. Doran's doorstep, Miles promised himself that he would never forget the affectionate good wishes with which they had parted from him. His last night in his lumpy bed was an uneasy one.

Mr. Barne was at the door punctually at eleven in the morning. Miles had spent some time packing, but he took only one small suitcase with him now. His shabby books, of which he was so fond, could be insinuated into his new magnificence later. He found Mr. Barne looking knowingly around Mrs. Doran's dark parlour, and said bluntly:

"You see that I have not been living in much style. It will be a very welcome change for me."

As they left the house Miles said:

"Tell me about the people in Dangan village. Who will my neighbours be?" He glanced sideways at the solicitor. "I intend to live at Dangan House, if I like it well enough."

"I'm sure you will like it," said Barne warmly. "There is quite a bit of company in the village. There is Tom Reid, an accountant here in Dublin, who goes up and down by car most days. He has a fine house there. There is Captain Merlin, and his daughter, Jane, a very pleasant young woman. And Miss Julia Hearn and her mother. They have a small house in the village. The mother is a cross old thing, but Miss Hearn is quite the opposite. Paul Walsh has the hotel. Martin Doyle is the manager of the mill—not much of a manager, but we can discuss that later. Oh, there are plenty of people. Tom Reid is very good company. He is not married," said Barne a trifle wistfully, Miles thought, "and he has plenty of time for amusement. You won't be dull at all."

"I don't expect I shall," said Miles gently, thinking of the long spell of dullness which he hoped to enjoy.

Mr. Barne's remarks had somehow not been very helpful. They gave him no more than a list of names. Their standards were different, he supposed, and he decided to reserve judgment until he could see for himself.

They were silent for most of the twenty-mile drive. Miles had not been outside the city for months, and he found himself intoxicated by the green of the trees and of the grass and growing corn. He was glad that Mr. Barne was content to watch the road, without so much as an occasional glance at the woods or tumbling streams as they passed. It was a cool, sunny day, sweet and clear as it can only be in early summer.

Dangan House, when he first caught sight of it, was utterly lovely. The gate was white-painted and unpretentious, set back a little from the road. The lodge, which was really a small house, was two-storied and covered in soft green Virginia creeper. There were delightful flower-beds before the lodge door, with tulips and forget-me-nots in bloom, and a light railing separating its little garden from the driveway. He did not need Barne's explanation that this was Germaine's house. A middle-aged woman in a white apron came out and opened the gate, and they drove through.

On either side of the drive, the parkland sloped gently upward. Oak trees were dotted here and there with careful artistry. Miles could not help thinking with infinite affection and respect of the visionary who had planted those trees, like walking-sticks, so long ago.

Half-way along the drive he asked Barne to stop for a moment and switch off the engine. He wanted to listen to the silence, so still at first, but then full of bird-calls and the bleating of sheep and lowing of cattle. Presently he pointed into the distant fields and asked:

"Do I see deer over there?"

"Jersey cattle," said Barne. "Cousins to deer. They are yours, too. I forgot to mention them. Sir Miles always kept about forty of them."

It was many, many years since there had been a cow in Miles's family. His bliss was now complete.

When they reached the house a few minutes later, he was surprised to find that it was built of cut limestone. It was L-shaped, and only two stories high. Around to the right he could see flower gardens and lawns. The drive went on past the house on the left, but the car turned in on to a wide gravel sweep before the door. There were wide stone steps and a heavy door of Irish oak. He was pleased to find the arms of the de Cogans, with the motto, carved above the lintel. The windows were broad and low and sunny, and the air was exquisitely scented with earth and grass and flowers.

Before they could reach the door, it was opened by a woman whom he took to be Mrs. Hooper. His heart sank at the sight of her, and he wondered how Barne had managed to convey a vision of a fat, motherly woman who would knit bed-socks for his birthday. The sad reality was thin in lumps, he thought, the way no one has a right to be thin. She looked soured with life, though just now she was trying to be pleasant. Her black dress and grey-streaked hair were neat but uninspired. Miles sighed a little as he answered her little speech of welcome.

Then she led them through the hall to a long drawing-room that looked out on the garden at the side of the house. It had a Persian carpet and an aged walnut grand piano, comfortable flowery armchairs, and tables at every suitable point. Its great limestone fireplace was the focal point of the whole room, with a portrait of a long-dead de Cogan hanging above. A small fire of logs burned in the grate. Miles liked its company, and tried not to remember Mrs. Doran's parlour fire, which had always been ruthlessly doused on the first of April. Though he was glad of Barne's support, still he wished that he were alone, so that he could walk excitedly up and down the room, like a small boy. He always felt like a small boy anyway, he excused himself, and moreover it was barely twenty-four hours since his whole life had changed.

Mr. Barne was saying, indicating the portrait:

"That is the Sir Miles de Cogan who came to Dangan first, in the sixteenth century, or so they say. Of course, this is not the original house. The site of that is a little further down the river."

"I thought I heard a river," said Miles. "Does it run through —my place?"

"Yes. We'll walk about after lunch. The back avenue leads to the village, and it crosses the river on its way. The main road from Dublin by-passes the village. If we had passed the front gate, we would have had to turn down to the left after a few hundred yards to get to the village—you'll see presently how it goes."

Miles was hardly listening, for he was at one of the side windows now, looking at the tulip-beds. He recollected himself with a sigh when Mrs. Hooper returned to conduct him upstairs to his room.

The stairs, carpeted in ecclesiastical purple, wound in a semicircle around the hall, and ended in a gallery from which long passage-ways stretched away on either side. Mrs. Hooper paused at the bedroom door nearest to the head of the stairs.

"I put you in here, Sir," she said. "It used to be Sir Miles's room. You could change later on, if you don't like it."

He was glad to hear the door shut behind him, as she led Barne off.

It was good to be alone at last. He walked slowly down the room. It was fully forty feet long, carpeted in soft grey, with brocaded curtains. The furniture was Hepplewhite, well cared for. A bookcase caught his eye, but he found that it contained nothing but bound copies of *The Field*. He reminded himself that it ill behoved him to scorn them, for he might learn from them how to look after his Jersey cows. He opened a door at the end of the room, and found himself in a yellow-fitted bathroom, carpeted in black. Monogrammed yellow towels hung on the hot rail. He raised his eyebrows, and came back into the middle of the room to think things out.

He had never envisaged anything like this. From the top of the stairs, surely he had seen doors into twenty rooms. At the end of one corridor, there had been a baize-covered door leading to servants' rooms. Downstairs, six doors had led out of the main hall, every one presumably opening into a room like the drawing-room in which he had been. He had thought of Dangan House as a Manor House, with perhaps five or six bedrooms and three or four sitting-rooms, as different from the reality as Mrs. Doran was from Mrs. Henley. Regretfully, he realized that he was too intelligent to reach out and grab it all for himself, without inquiring further into his moral right of ownership. The fact that he was madly, despairingly in love with it only made his obligation more imperative. His very suitcase, cringing like an interloper beside the bed, seemed to agree with him.

As he dried his hands on the yellow towel, he reflected that he should have known that he could not have remained in a state of simple happiness, like a child with new toys on Christmas morning. The trouble was that he had not realized that people still lived in such style, and the feeling of discomfort that he felt could almost be called embarrassment. It was as if he had blundered on to the stage in the middle of a play about gentlemen of leisure. And naturally he feared that the actors would resent his presence. He wondered if he should mention his fears to Mr. Barne, and ask for advice on his attitude towards his cousin, Germaine. Obviously, she should have been the owner of all this, if her brother had not cut her off.

There were newly-washed, silver-backed brushes on the

dressing-table, each with the capering figure of a little goat engraved on the back. Miles knew that a goat figured in the coat of arms over the door.

"How appropriate," he thought, remembering the goat-like face in the photograph that Barne had shown him.

He brushed his hair vigorously with the brushes, with apologies to Sir Miles, in case his ghost happened to be watching. He imagined that a little sound like a sigh went through the room, and he wished that he had not been so irreverent. He left the room at last, and went downstairs to wait for Barne.

3

Feeling very bold, Miles opened one of the doors near the foot of the stairs. He found himself in a pleasant library, furnished with a moss-green carpet and leather chairs and sofas. There were book-shelves on one wall only, and he started eagerly to look over the titles. What he saw filled him with depression. It was all too obvious that his cousin had been no reader. There were gardening and farming books, to be sure, and a few works on farm machinery, but literature was represented by the hide-bound works of Dickens, suspiciously clean, and a few well-worn, ancient school stories of the 1890s. The horrid thought crossed Miles's mind that these last had been the staple reading of their owner for some fifty years. He was sadly disappointed. That strange, little face with its rabbity grin could have betokened an impish, lively mind, with the infuriating quality of a midge on a summer night. The reality, however, seemed to have been banal in the extreme, or at best lazy and inert. At this point in his reflections Barne came into the room, saying:

"So you have found the books. What do you think of them?"

"Very nice," said Miles politely. "They give me a certain insight into the mind of my cousin."

"I can't say that I read much myself," said Barne.

Miles looked at him with surprise, and forbore from asking him what he did in the long winter evenings. Barne went on:

"Sir Miles was an exacting person, in many ways. He did not suffer fools gladly, and he had a principle that there is one right way for doing everything. He could see no reason why anything should ever be done wrong. You will see evidences of this everywhere. The farm was perfectly run, the gardens kept in perfect order, the servants perfectly trained. But he was no business man. He left all that to me—income-tax, wages, rents, rates and so on."

"And the mill?" asked Miles.

"Martin Doyle manages everything there, including the accounts," said Barne. "The mill is not doing much. I should advise you to get rid of it. You might find a business man who would be interested—Tom Reid, for instance."

But some instinct in Miles reacted against this suggestion. He liked the idea of owning the mill, and was even pleased, in a strange way, to hear that it was not doing well. Here would be some useful work to do, to build it up and expand it, and through it to earn the right to live like a king in Dangan House. He tried to explain some of this to Barne, but he soon gave up. He could see that Barne thought that anyone who wanted to work when he could be idle was a fool. He asked a question or two about the manager, and what commission he had on the profits.

"He has a good salary," said Barne. "Five hundred a year and a free house. Living is cheap out here in the country. Sir Miles was old fashioned about these things. Doyle did ask for a commission but he would not give it to him."

"That was a pity," said Miles. "It should have made him work harder, as well as making him more contented and happy."

Presently Mrs. Hooper announced lunch, and they went into the dining-room. Seated one on either side of a Nelson table, they had an excellent meal, served by a thin man in a white jacket. Miles remembered his manners, and tried not to say "Thank you" too often, but by the time the meal was over, he had begun to feel the strain. He noticed that Barne ate up everything very happily. Later they went back to the drawing-room and smoked cigars from a box on the table beside the fire. Barne handed them to Miles, who found himself irrationally irritated that the other should think it necessary to play the host. Looking through the sweet, blue smoke, he said:

"This is on a much bigger scale than I had imagined."

"Do you like it?"

"It is quite delightful," said Miles simply. "But I wonder who should be here instead of me. Is Germaine sitting down in the lodge now, biting her nails and hoping that the fairies will take me?"

Barne laughed heartily.

"If she is, I don't see why you should lose any sleep," he said. "I advise you to keep far away from her. She's a real old maid, meddlesome and talkative, and she has no reason to love you." He hesitated a little and then went on: "I had meant to bring up this question. I think it might be very well if you could come to an arrangement with her to leave the lodge and go to live somewhere else. You could afford to make a cash settlement."

Miles said:

"I'll think about that."

He had already decided that it would be better to wait until he had met Germaine. After all, he reasoned, he was an old maid himself, so it was quite possible that there would be some affinity between them. He thought he would wait until Barne would have gone back to Dublin, because only then would he feel free to make an independent judgment. At the back of his mind, he was beginning to regret having asked Barne to stay the night. It was subtly apparent that the little man thought he needed a great deal of guidance on personal relationships. He supposed that Barne had formed his conclusions from the few minutes that he had spent in Mrs. Doran's parlour. It was too late now to wish that he had met him at the office. Barne had not asked, and Miles had not told him how he had earned his living during all those years in Dublin. He chuckled to himself as he remembered last night's party in Canning Street.

"What is so amusing?" asked Barne in surprise.

"Just remembering my former greatness," said Miles. "Shall we go out and walk about?"

They went out of the front door and turned into the avenue that led around to the side of the house. There was wistaria on the wall there, already in bud. The avenue was sanded, and bore the tracks of metal-rimmed wheels, and of horses' hooves. Farther on there was a tall, wooden farm-yard gate, standing open. Inside, some brown plus-foured hens—Miles's hens!— were pecking among the cobbles. They went into the yard, and he saw coach-houses at the far side, with double doors wide enough to take a carriage. There were two cars there now, and Barne led him across to look at them. But Miles was smelling the sweet, leathery smell of carriages, that no amount of petrol could mask. It brought him back, with a swift intolerable rush, to his youth, so that sudden tears came into his eyes. He stepped out again into the sunlight, and went across to look into the stables. They were empty, but Barne, at his elbow, told him that the two farm horses were out working.

"There are a couple of saddle horses as well," he said. "Sir Miles liked to ride about the farm. They are quiet old things, John says."

"Just like me," said Miles. "Are they out on grass?"

"I suppose so."

They left the yard and followed the avenue until it crossed a hump-backed bridge. Miles leaned on the stone parapet and looked down into the tumbling, grey-brown water, feeling the unappreciative presence of Barne at his elbow. Green fields bordered the river on either side, and looking upstream, he could see the land open out into a wide prospect of meadows and cornfields. Behind him the river took a turn and disappeared among trees, and down there he could hear the creak of a mill-wheel.

Beyond the bridge the avenue crossed a wide, grassy, tree-fringed field, and ended at a five-barred farm-gate, with a small lodge at one side. Barne explained that Matt Murphy, the head gardener, lived there. They passed through the gate and turned to the right, and almost at once they were at the top of the village street.

"You see," said Barne unnecessarily, "the village lies between your two gates——"

Miles hardly heard him. He was enchanted with the village, for it was the most charming one that he had ever seen. Such villages usually have an air of decay, he thought, as if the feudal purpose for which they were built could not be concealed. The *grand seigneur* must have servants, so he builds a village with picturesque houses and dingy serfs. Though Dangan village had probably been built in the same spirit, it had a character and vitality of its own. Most of the houses were in good repair, painted freshly and embellished with blossoming window-boxes. There were several prosperous-looking shops, and a well-kept hotel half-way down the street. Near them, where they stood, the little mill rumbled, and floury men walked about with sacks. Now Miles could see the mill-race, and the huge wheel slowly and benevolently turning. He had no doubt that it was the presence of the mill that made this village different. Opposite the mill, the Catholic church stood a little back from the footpath. It was painted white, and its low, slated porch looked like a single eyebrow.

"Could we go into the mill?" he asked.

But when they reached the doorway, a tall fair-haired young man came out. He stopped dead when he saw them, and his face went blank. Barne introduced him coldly as Mr. Doyle, and then walked a pace or two away, leaving them alone together. Miles affected not to notice, and presently the young man softened enough to give him a peep at his mill. Miles ended by asking him to call a few evenings later, and then he strolled after Barne.

"I didn't know that you were actually unfriendly with Mr. Doyle," he said bluntly.

"It's all on his side," said Barne with a tolerant shrug. "He's

32

a stupid young man. I have given up trying to placate him. In my profession one makes many enemies," he added with a grin.

As they walked down the street as far as the hotel, Miles was conscious of eyes watching him from doors and windows. It was an uncomfortable sensation, though he did not think they were hostile eyes. He was glad enough when Barne suggested that they go into the hotel and meet the landlord.

"It's not a big hotel," Barne said, "about ten bedrooms, usually inhabited by fishing colonels. Dangan is a quiet place—there is nothing here to attract noisy people."

This last remark was overheard by a middle-aged man who emerged from the dimness at the back of the hall. He was hatchet-faced, and had a wild growth of curly, grey hair. A large white apron covered his paunch and was tied with pathetic little strings at the back. He grunted at Barne, but affected not to see Miles at all, as he led the way into the bar. Behind the counter he barked:

"Well, what'll it be?"

They had small whiskies, and after the first sip, Barne said:

"Is the boss at home, Joe?"

"Gone to town. I heard what you said just now. Sounds like you didn't hear the latest."

"What's that? Tell us."

"Ah, that'd be telling!" said Joe lugubriously. He shot a sideways look at Miles. "Glad to meet you, Mr. de Cogan, Sir."

Miles, startled, made some reply. Joe went on with gloomy satisfaction:

"The boss is hopping mad, but there's nothing he can do, and so I told him. 'There's nothing at all you can do, Mr. Walsh,' I said, 'and you might as well make up your mind to it. The country is gone to the dogs,' I said, 'with lassies on bicycles and young blackguards chasing after them in cars, and the whole lot of them lapping up the drink like it was new milk.'"

Miles took an appreciative lap out of his glass and grinned

gently into it. He had often heard Joe's grievance expounded before, but usually with less venom. Barne sighed at the depravity of modern youth and said:

"True enough, Joe. What made you say all that?"

"Ah, wait a while, gentlemen—that's all I say! Wait a while! Dangan is a nice quiet little spot now. But just wait! Our mothers and our sisters and our daughters and aunts and—and female cousins can go out for a nice little walk for themselves in the evenings now, without us sitting at home worrying about them. But just wait until Mr. Reid builds his new road-house at the cross—and there won't be an innocent girl this side of the Sally Gap!"

"Good gracious!" said Barne. "A road-house?"

"That's what he called it, sir. I heard it with my own two ears." He wagged them expertly to show which two ears he meant. "Right here in this bar."

"Perhaps it will be a quiet place," said Miles soothingly.

"Not if Mr. Reid can help it," said Joe. "A shiny bar and enough bottles to intoxicate a herd of elephants and blondes with brass necks sitting around at little tables looking sociable —that's what he's planning. A natural development, he called it. But you may be sure that it will develop a packet of money into his own pocket." Suddenly he began to polish the bar excitedly, and his tone changed to one of respectful admiration. "Oh, a fine business man and no mistake. 'Tisn't everyone would see the possibilities of Dangan—a quiet, sleepy little place, as you might say, with nothing going on in it——"

"Good afternoon, Tom," said Barne with quiet enjoyment.

Miles became aware that a big man had just come in, and was undoubtedly the cause of Joe's embarrassment.

"Joe has been telling us about your new road-house," Barne went on. "It was the first I had heard of it. By the way, this is Mr. de Cogan, your new neighbour. Mr. Reid."

He looked anxiously from one to the other, and Miles felt a pang of sympathy for him. He so obviously wanted them to like each other, as a man does when he introduces to each other two of his friends. Tom Reid was shaking Miles's hand affably and welcoming him to Dangan as if the whole place belonged to him. Miles smiled sweetly and thanked him, contriving, he hoped, to give the impression that this was the happiest day of his life. But he had recognized Mr. Reid at once as a type which he disliked. He supposed that such people fitted somewhere into God's scheme of things, but for the life of him he could not think where.

Tom Reid was well over six feet tall. The very best of good feeding from the hour of his birth had built him up broad in proportion. He had a great big sleek head, and large grey eyes that protruded slightly. His forehead was high, and sheltered, Miles guessed, a fat, selfish brain like a summer slug under a wet stone. Barne had said that he was a bachelor, but Miles could see that by rights he should have had a big, fat, well-conditioned wife to match. His collar and tie lay flat and smooth on his beautiful pale shirt, and he wore a fawn-coloured overcoat over his perfectly pressed suit.

"Double-breasted suit, for sure," thought Miles, and was pleased to find himself right in his guess.

Men like these have their clothing cowed, he thought. Their collars would never dare to develop a wrinkle.

"What do you think of the road-house plan?" Reid asked, and went on without waiting for an answer: "I've bought that little three-cornered field at the cross-roads from old Mrs. Daly. I gave her two hundred quid for it—enough to keep her for the rest of her life. She thought it was worth nothing, but I wouldn't let that stop me from giving her a fair price."

Miles reflected that Reid probably thought that he had bought the goodwill of the whole village with the same two hundred pounds. Joe had gone down to the end of the bar, where he was polishing glasses with exaggerated industry. His hunched shoulders somehow suggested the disapproval that he would not have dared to show in his face.

35

"Do you think the people in the village will like it?" asked Barne gently.

"They'll like it soon enough, when their daughters get jobs there," said Reid. "I'm a great believer in barmaids."

He winked meaningly in the direction of Joe. Barne smiled appreciatively, but Miles did not. He thought it was mean of Reid to tease Joe, who had been polite enough to try to hide his feelings. Reid was not finished yet. He called out, in an affected drawl:

"Hey, Joe! You're one of those people whose daughters can have jobs. I've already promised one to your daughter Nora."

Joe stopped polishing, and half-turned, as he said softly:

"When did you do that, Mr. Reid?"

"I met her just now, in the street. She said she has no job yet."

"She has plenty of time," said Joe quickly. "Plenty of time."

"Yes, she'll be just ready about the time my road-house is built," said Reid.

Miles put out a hand, as if he would stop the trend of the conversation with it. Joe had gone white in the face. He moved up behind the counter, until he was directly opposite to Reid. Then he said shakily:

"Mr. Reid, sir, are you making ugly suggestions about my daughter Nora?"

"He asked for it," thought Miles, in despair at being present at such a scene. "He asked for it, the great, thick, stupid worm!"

Some of the hatred he had aroused penetrated to Reid. He laughed nervously.

"Of course not—I mean, what I said was the opposite. You've got the wrong end of the stick altogether."

"Have I, now?" murmured Joe. "I wonder have I?" He leaned forward a little and said softly: "It's well for you if I have. If I thought you made an ugly suggestion about my daughter Nora, I would wipe you off the face of the earth— like that!"

He swept his hand along the counter, and sent a glass on to the floor, where it exploded with a little crash. There was silence for a moment, and then Barne pulled at Reid's sleeve. Miles finished his drink meditatively. Joe was looking stupidly at the broken glass on the floor.

Miles expected Reid to react with threats in his turn, and, sure enough, his injured dignity rose to the occasion. He called Joe an insolent servant, among other things, all of them out of place in democratic Ireland. He also swore that Joe would be disemployed without delay. Miles squirmed with embarrassment for him. He used theatrical phrases and gestures quite unsuited to the education of Joe, who hardly seemed to be listening anyhow. He ended by prancing out of the bar, followed by Barne, and a moment later by Miles, who could not resist murmuring first:

"Good man, Joe!"

As he left the bar he saw Joe lean into a drawer under the counter for a small box. He opened it and flicked a white tablet into his mouth.

4

On the steps of the hotel, Miles found Reid still stamping and chattering. Barne was now plucking at his sleeve in his efforts to soothe him down. Miles said gently:

"Dangan is such a quiet place, Mr. Reid. I'm sure people will begin to look this way in a moment."

He stepped on to the footpath, noticing that Reid had immediately resumed control of himself. Obviously he could have stopped himself much sooner, if he had wanted. They walked along the street together, and now Miles noticed that the curious glances that reached them were undoubtedly hostile as well. Barne greeted acquaintances on either side, but he did not introduce Miles to anyone.

At the far end of the village a wrought-iron gate stood open on a carriage-drive. Reid said casually, only betraying his pride by a lift of his huge head:

"Would you like to come in and see my little place? It's nothing like yours, of course, de Cogan," he added.

Miles said quickly that he would be pleased to go in. As they walked up the drive, Reid explained that he had owned the place for a mere four years, and he pointed out the improvements that he had carried out in the grounds. Undergrowth had been cleared away, trees thinned, bulbs planted and grass levelled. Miles almost began to like him, as he showed them one feature after another. Then he realized that this was not the delight of an artist in his creation, but that Reid was simply thumping his chest again, and telling him what a fine clever fellow he was. The drive was short, and in a few minutes they reached the house.

It was a lovely Georgian house, flat and clean-lined, with an austerity and sophistication about it which did not accord with its owner. Still, Reid was patently delighted with it, and he led them briskly inside as if he were a child about to display the wonders of a doll's house. No reserve, thought Miles disapprovingly.

They went into a square drawing-room on the right of the door. It was well furnished in classic taste, but Miles could not forbear a satisfied smirk when he saw the pictures. They bore out his judgment of Reid with appalling force.

"I had him sized up, all right," he said to himself, with awful joy.

There were five pictures altogether, each one more excruciating than the last. They were framed in shiny gold, and showed colourful, stout, biblical ladies sitting at wells leering at their inward thoughts, and stupid-looking, purple-faced men sitting in abandoned attitudes around meaty dinner tables. Each picture had a caption, and Miles went around and solemnly read them all. Then he became frightened, lest Reid might ask him what he thought of them.

But Reid had immediately begun to pour out drinks.

"He's like a car—must be fuelled often," said Miles to himself, and refused the whisky that he was offered.

He was quite unaccustomed to drinking spirits, and the one drink that he had had at the hotel was even now sending a bold little devil cruising about inside him. He was having difficulty enough in controlling it, and he feared that at any moment he might betray the unkind thoughts that were in his mind. Reid was saying:

"Won't you have anything at all?" Miles shook his head.

"Some tea? Yes, you'll have some tea."

Miles hated tea. But Reid's finger was on the bell and a moment later he was ordering tea from a scuttling manservant.

"I'd scuttle myself, if I worked for Reid," thought Miles, and resigned himself to the tea.

It came on a heavy silver tray, with buns and cakes and little sandwiches. Reid obviously enjoyed the sight of his man pouring and handing cups. He sat with a child-like smile on his face, and made no attempt to help. The trouble was, Miles reflected, that what is attractive in a child is often the reverse in an adult.

"Miles," he said to himself as he sipped his tea, "you are going to be a horrible old man."

Suddenly Reid glanced towards the window, and amazingly blushed to the roots of his sleek hair. Barne, who was selecting a sandwich, did not notice anything amiss. Reid got up and went out, mumbling an apology, and a moment later he came back leading a young girl, whose every movement he watched with unashamed devotion.

She could have been no more than twenty, and she was as frightened as a cat. She was small and lightly built, with a lovely delicate little head and little, square, slightly uplifted chin. She wore no hat, and her hair was cut straight across like a child's. It was reddish-gold hair, soft and wavy, and like a cloud of gold-dust. It was no wonder to Miles that Reid was captivated by her. He doubted, though, if Reid were capable of seeing her unique mixture of helplessness and determination, of physical frailty and mental strength. Out of her childish face looked as intelligent a pair of navy-blue eyes as he ever hoped to see. But she was frightened of Reid, and angry with him, too. He pawed her arm a little as he introduced her to the company.

"Miss Jane Merlin, my little neighbour," he said, looking at her sideways.

Miles and Barne had leaped to their feet as she came in. She knew Barne already, it seemed. She welcomed Miles to Dangan with a maturity of phrase far beyond her years. He guessed her mother was dead—possibly both parents. But then she turned to Reid and handed him a letter which she had been carrying in her hand.

"This is from my father," she said.

She had a slight nervous impediment in her speech, and her head jerked a little as she spoke. Miles felt a twitch of anger go through him. What sort of father was this, he wondered, who had allowed his charming little daughter to get into such a state? He was certain that it need not have happened to such an intelligent girl. In their small community, no doubt, it would not be long before he would discover the reason of it. Meanwhile, he determined to make friends with Miss Merlin, if she would let him.

She accepted a cup of tea from Reid, determinedly choosing a small straight chair at the far side of the room, and addressing most of her conversation to Miles. Reid looked on proudly from the sofa, and did not seem to mind. All at once, Miles realized that the expression on his face was the same as when he had asked them to come in and look at the house. Pride of possession, that's what it was! It was clear enough to Miles now that Reid wanted Miss Merlin to complete the picture of his house. "What is home without a mother", in fact. The nerve of the man! Quite sobered now, Miles felt that he needed his tea, and he drank it to the last drop.

Presently they got up to go. Jane Merlin said that she would go with them, and for all Reid's coy persuasiveness she insisted on her decision. At last he gave in indulgently, as who should say:

"Very well, you may have your way now. But when I have control, you shall do everything according to my pleasure."

He came to the door with them, and watched them down the avenue with a pleased smirk on his face.

They left Jane at the gate of a small gabled house, the last in the village. An eight-foot stone wall separated Reid's little estate from her pretty garden. As they walked back through the village Barne said:

"Well, what do you think of Reid?"

Remembering that Barne had seemed to like him, Miles answered cautiously:

"He seems a very affable fellow."

"He is," said Barne eagerly. "That's a fine place he has there. You have no idea how much he has improved it. It was a wilderness when he took it over."

Miles was able to say with sincerity that it was very well kept now. He made no reference to the scene that Reid had made at the hotel. Barne went on:

"He loves Dangan. He spends all the time he can here—he even brings down some of his work so that he does not have to go to town every day. Oh, you'll see a lot of him. And he's all for improving the village—you'll find that that is why he wants to build the road-house. It will give employment, and it will remind Dublin people that Dangan exists. It's a real little beauty spot, don't you agree?"

Miles agreed, with a sigh. Then he remembered his two-hundred-acre estate, and assured himself that if Dangan ever became the haunt of city people, he would put up a series of notices saying: "Beware of Bull." This reminded him to ask:

"By the way, do I own a bull?"

"Yes," said Barne, staring. "A Jersey bull."

But this did not sound menacing enough at all. A Jersey bull—a bull in a jersey—it was quite undignified. He giggled, and Barne stared still more. Miles said hurriedly:

"It takes time to get used to owning a bull. Have I a land steward as well?"

"Oh, yes. John Wall. An old man, but knows his business through and through. He oversees the farm and gardens and all. His father and grandfather were here before him."

As they passed the post office, Mr. Barne said in a low voice:

"Your Mrs. Hooper's sister is the post-mistress. She is a Miss Byrne—a very friendly sort of person. Would you like to come in and see her?"

But Miles felt suddenly tired, and he said that he would like to go home. There would be plenty of time for meeting all those people later on.

Beyond the post office, however, he paused again, to ask Barne about a tiny house that stood back a little from the street, with a small dank square of garden in front. The row of houses on either side shut off the light from the garden, so that nothing would grow there except a few depressed little laurel bushes, and the moss that pushed its way up between the flags of the path. The house had small dark windows, two upstairs and one on either side of the worn door. The only spark of life was the little polished brass knocker. It was like finding a dead body in one's path, and it affected Miles deeply.

"Who lives there?" he asked. "Surely that is not one of my houses."

"No, no. That house belongs to Reid, in fact." Barne looked uncomfortable. "It's pretty bleak, all right. It's not a very old house, but it was built at a bad time. He has let it to Miss Julia Hearn and her mother. I think I mentioned them to you. Miss Hearn used to be a singer, I've heard. They are very poor, and I suppose they find it cheap to live in Dangan."

Miles made Barne point out his own houses, and he was relieved to find that they were all solid little slate-roofed cottages, well painted and cheerful-looking. Still, he knew his conscience would force him to visit every one of them, and the prospect alarmed him. He would wait until Barne had gone, of course, so he had a breathing-space for a day or two.

The mill was still working when they passed it on their way home. In the evening silence it seemed to hum louder, like a fat, contented bee. The sun was still able to look under the trees as they turned in at the back gate. On the bridge, Miles paused to look up the river at the quiet fields. To-morrow he would walk along its banks and find out where the river came from.

In the big cobbled yard they heard the hum of a milking-machine. Miles looked into the byre where a long double line of Jersey cows stood munching. Marvellous tubes took the milk from them while they stood there quite unconcerned. The nearest cow looked at Miles with big, round eyes. She had long curled eyelashes. She was like a film star, he thought, with her beautiful, simple expression and flawless complexion. His cow —his forty cows. It certainly was odd.

Barne had remained outside the door because, he said, he did not like the smell. Miles walked bravely down between the square ends of the cows to introduce himself to an old man who was supervising the milking at the far end of the byre. This was John Wall, the steward, and he spent a happy ten minutes explaining to Miles how the milking-machine worked. He was a tall man, and he held himself as straight as a wheat-stalk. His white hair and the careful precision with which he walked were the only signs of his age. He was obviously devoted to his cows and to his machine. He looked Miles over keenly, with the privilege of an old man, and at last he said:

"Sir Miles was always very fond of his cows. Nothing was too good for their comfort."

Miles said gravely and gently that he had never owned cows before now, but that it seemed to him that such hard-working beasts deserved nothing but the best.

He rejoined Barne, who was waiting for him rather unhappily among the hens, and they went into the house.

Miles found himself refreshed by the little interval alone in his room before dinner. There were many new people to be considered and adjustments to be made in his own point of view. He was glad to find that he was not too old to learn. Another five years and he would have been quite uneasy without Mrs. Doran's chains.

Already, plans for the future were beginning to take shape in his mind. To begin with, Mrs. Hooper was for the axe. She was a very worthy woman, perhaps, but she reminded him too much of the lady in *The Fall of the House of Ussher*. She was like a reheated corpse, as Mrs. Henley would say. Apart from her depressing appearance, he had a feeling that she would very soon begin to bully him, and with a considerable chance of success. She had the eye of a priest's housekeeper. She would make him dress for dinner, and read *The Field*, and shoot whatever creatures the gentlemen were shooting at the time of year. In short, she gave him an inferiority complex. How to manage without her was another problem. Barne had said that she was a good housekeeper. His heart failed him for a moment. Then, striking an attitude before the wardrobe glass, he quoted Shaw's Saint Joan:

"I will dare and dare and dare until I die!"

He began to wonder about Jane Merlin, and why she seemed frightened of Reid. He could not believe that she was a timid girl. The fact that she showed her dislike of Reid so plainly went to prove that she was not timid, but she looked cornered. Yes, that was the word.

Over dinner he made Barne talk about Captain Merlin. He had lived in Dangan for years, Barne said. He hardly ever left the village. He was something of an oddity, spending most of the day sitting in the little drawing-room of his house, reading newspapers and writing quantities of letters. In the evenings he would take a walk through the village, sometimes dropping into the hotel bar for a pint of Guinness with a shot of rum in it. The village people tolerated him, though they laughed at him, too. He was always dressed in a grey tweed knickerbocker suit of uncertain age, and it was commonly said that one would not know whether the Captain were going or coming, but for the patch on the seat of his trousers.

"And the daughter?" Miles prodded.

Barne shrugged.

"It's hard on a pretty little girl to have a father like that. She takes after her mother, I have heard. She was away at school until a couple of years ago, when she came home to look after the old man."

"She looks nervous," said Miles.

"I'm sure her father is a trial to live with," said Barne. "But you may have noticed that Tom Reid is taking an interest in

45

her?" Miles nodded. "That would be good for her. Reid is a fine prosperous fellow, and it's time he got married and settled down. Perhaps all she needs is a little security and affection. Reid would give her that. He would look after her properly— let her dress well and run up and down to Dublin, and have a car of her own. That's what she needs."

It was a point of view, Miles supposed. But if things turned out as Barne suggested, it would not be surprising if Jane became hard-faced, hard-drinking and soured. Then, no doubt, Reid would feel cheated, and would never understand what had happened. Miles sighed at this prospect.

They spent the evening in the library, over maps of the estate. Miles tried to ask one or two intelligent questions, and was rewarded with a maddeningly detailed inventory of his new property. He could not become interested in it until he had seen more of it. By the time they had done he was exhausted, though he was careful not to show it. He spent another restless night, but in spite of that he awoke with a curious feeling of peace. Barne was leaving to-day, and from now on he would be alone.

5

Still, a full week had passed before Miles felt really free. He spent the time in rambling about the farm, sometimes going for a walk through the village or the lanes near by. He discovered that it was the business of James MacDonagh, the efficient man who waited at table, to drive him about if he so wished, and he went for one or two excursions into the hinterland. James always began by being very stiff and proper, dressing for his part in leather gaiters and knee-breeches, and shutting Miles firmly into the back seat. But once they were on the road he softened out and told anecdotes about the village people and the people in the big houses that they passed, until Miles felt that he knew as much about them as if he had lived in Dangan all his life. Sometimes James would say apologetically:

"Of course you'll understand, Sir, 'tis not backbiting the decent people I am, but in a place like Dangan you have to know all about your neighbours or you couldn't live at all."

It was he who told Miles that the village people hated Reid. It was hard to say why, except that he had rubbed them the wrong way from the day of his arrival. He lorded it over them, as Miles had seen, and they resented this all the more because someone had found out that his father had been a blacksmith in a County Limerick village. Miles said that it was an extraordinary achievement for a poor boy to have turned himself into an accountant. James agreed, with a shrug. But it seemed that Reid had affected a knowledge of horses, and this was thought to be the last straw.

"Well, he probably did know something about horses," thought Miles, "if his father was a blacksmith."

And he felt a pang of pity for the young Reid, helping in the forge while long-nosed persons on tall horses looked down on him. Living among the big stud-farms of Limerick would be enough to give a fixation about horses to a less self-conscious man than Reid. He asked:

"Does Reid have horses in Dangan?"

"Oh, yes. He rides well, too," said James grudgingly. "He's a fine sight on a horse, there's no one can deny."

It was three days before Miles summoned enough courage to visit Germaine. He had not even seen her yet. Except for the days when he had swept through in style in his Bentley, he had not used the front gate at all. He knew that this could not go on for ever, but he had weakly avoided facing the embarrassment of meeting her for the first time. Perhaps it was not weakness, after all, but the realization that delicacy and tact almost beyond his power were required. At last he came to a decision. He would approach Germaine determinedly, and if she showed any sign at all of understanding his difficulties, he would bluntly put his proposition to her and risk the rest. If she were already cold and resentful, his visit could hardly make things worse. He remembered Barne's description of her—meddlesome and talkative.

So with his heart pounding he walked down the avenue on his third afternoon in Dangan. It was almost four o'clock, and as he stood on Germaine's sunny little porch after he had knocked, he had a moment of panic lest she might have gone out. If she were, the anticlimax would be harder to bear than all his built-up fears. But the door was opened by the white-aproned woman whose business it seemed to be to look after the gates, too. She opened her mouth with excited pleasure. Miles asked if Miss de Cogan were at home.

"Oh, yes, Sir. Yes, indeed. I mean, come in, Sir, into the room, and I'll get her——"

She fluttered behind him and all around him as she conducted him into a room off the hall. It was small, but still very

48

restful, with an economy of decoration which showed its pleasant proportions to good advantage. The small-paned window framed the tulip-beds and the rising green fields beyond the avenue. Through the partly opened door he could hear the maid's excited voice saying:

"It's Mr. de Cogan, Miss. It is indeed. Well, I got the surprise of my life—I didn't know whether to bring him in or not."

"Thank you, Sally," a cool voice interrupted her. "You did quite right."

A moment later Germaine came into the room. She stood uncertainly with her back to the door, while she examined him. Then she came towards him with her hand outstretched and said:

"You are my cousin Miles. How nice of you to come."

Holding her hand in his for a moment Miles felt a wave of pleasure go through him. He said tentatively:

"I should have come before——"

Then he stopped to look at her. She was older than he was—perhaps nearly sixty. Her iron-grey hair was worn long, and rolled into an old-fashioned bun. There was an obvious likeness to her brother, as Miles had seen him in Barne's photograph, but her blue-grey eyes were gentle and friendly, with a distinct spark of humour. She was small, but like many small women she looked more than capable of defending herself. It seemed incredible that she should have gone so far in her difference with her brother as to leave his house. Miles wondered if he would ever hear the whole story of that quarrel.

Presently they were sitting at a low table drinking tea, brought by the beaming Sally, while Germaine asked him what he thought of Dangan. She sighed a little at his enthusiastic reply and said:

"Yes, it is a delightful place, I hope you'll be very happy."

Miles seized the moment to say:

"I have heard that you used to live at the house." He drew a long breath, and in an agony of embarrassment heard his own voice go on. "Please don't think it is an impertinence. I came to ask you—if you would come back and live there again."

At last it was out. Through a red fog he saw her raised eyebrows and the amusement dawning at the corners of her mouth. She said gently:

"Please don't be so distressed. You needn't be afraid of me."

"I've been very untactful," he groaned. "Please forget I said anything about it."

"That would be silly," she said briskly, "after all your pain in saying what you want. Have you thought it all out? You're only here three days, you know."

A sensible woman, too, thank God, thought Miles, as his brain began to clear again.

"I have thought about it," he said earnestly. "Barne told me that you used to keep house, and that it was only after you had gone that Mrs. Hooper came. So if you were to come back it would be quite proper to ask Mrs. Hooper to go. Now I'm saying much worse things." He mopped his forehead with his hand. "Mrs. Hooper reminds me so much of my old landlady in Dublin," he finished appealingly.

How Barne would disapprove of this! He wondered for a second if he were making a terrible mistake in trusting his own judgment more than the advice of the solicitor, who had known Germaine for so many years. He was reassured to find that Germaine doubted the wisdom of the idea, too. It took time and lengthy discussion before she at last agreed to come. She did not tell him why she had left the big house and had come to live in the lodge, but she stipulated that if the arrangement became irksome to either of them, she would leave again.

"I liked living here," she said, looking around the little room. "The traffic on the road bothered me at first, and the fact that Sally was never more than a few feet away from me, but one becomes accustomed to these things in time."

"Would it be proper to give Mrs. Hooper a pension?" Miles asked as he stood up to go.

He was relieved when Germaine agreed that this would be a

good idea, for he was beginning to understand the fearfulness of the task that he had brought on himself. Obviously, no one but he could break the news of her dismissal to Mrs. Hooper. Before he left, he arranged with Germaine to come up to the house after dinner.

Mrs. Hooper was surprisingly difficult. He sent for her before dinner, and explained to her that he intended to go back to the old arrangement whereby Germaine kept house, and that therefore there would be no further work for her. He would like to compensate her, however, with a small pension of five pounds a month, and hoped that they would part friends. He had reeled off all of this carefully prepared speech before he noticed the change in her. She stood before him, stiff and thin in her black dress, like a witch about to curse an enemy. All the venom concentrated in her sharp yellow face should have ossified him where he stood. Her eyes were pin-pointed and shining, and her lank hair seemed to him to writhe like a sparse bundle of snakes. She thrust her head forward and bent her shoulders, and then she advanced on him with a sort of flat-footed goose-step, until her face was only a few inches away from his. Embarrassed for her, he tried to turn aside, but she misunderstood his motive.

"So you can't look me in the face, me fine gentleman!" she hissed. "No wonder, and you after being warned!"

"I'm afraid I don't understand you," said Miles. "I think it would be better not to discuss it any more."

" 'Tis not discussing it at all I am," she said softly. "Maybe you don't know I have friends. Maybe you don't know that you can't put me out of my job so easy. If everyone knew what I know——"

She stopped suddenly. Miles said sharply:

"Go on. What do you know?"

Suddenly she was frightened.

"I'm sorry, Mr. de Cogan, Sir. I don't know what came over me. Oh, why didn't I keep my mouth shut?"

And she burst into an ugly fit of weeping. Miles, who wished for nothing better than that she should keep her mouth shut, patted her on the shoulder and said:

"Now, don't worry about it at all, Mrs. Hooper. We'll forget the whole thing. I can see that you were very much upset, and I'm sorry for it."

So with easy phrases he got her out of the room, and came back to the fire to think about what she had said and to wonder what was behind it all. She had given him one hint at what he took to be the common talk of the village, and it had shocked him deeply. He knew that this was silly, of course. He had expected the veiled contempt that is usually felt for the *nouveau riche*, but until now his new acquaintances had either covered their feelings well or had been genuinely friendly and charitable. All at once he had a vision of the houses with their roofs lifted off, so that he could see venomous little groups of villagers inside, all talking about him, and probably hoping that he would make blunders enough to provide them with more gossip. In his ensuing misery he longed for Germaine's arrival, and yet a small inner voice now cautioned him again not to trust her either. He sighed for the rose-coloured spectacles he had worn until this evening.

When Germaine came, he watched her sharply for a few minutes, but he had to admit that he could find nothing wrong with her attitude. He told her something of his fears, and she answered with the well-worn proverb:

"You can't please all the people all the time."

"You think that Mrs. Hooper was only talking vaguely?"

"She must have been discussing you with her sister and her friends in the village. It takes time for these people to develop loyalties. When they become accustomed to you, they will soon tire of talking about you. You give a certain amount of employment to the village people. On the whole they will be well disposed towards you."

"Why don't you feel ill-will towards me?" Miles asked curiously.

52

"Because I'm old enough to know better," said Germaine briskly. "Don't forget that I gave up my interest in this house several years ago."

Miles felt almost quite consoled by this. They spent the evening in the drawing-room, and he talked to Germaine about his youth. Places and incidents that he had deliberately forgotten now crowded into his mind. She listened to it all with quiet sympathy, and encouraged him to fill in more detail.

"I always wondered about you," she said. "But my father would never tell me anything. Once when I was nearly grown up, he and my brother Miles met your father, and I thought we were all going to be friends at last. But nothing came of it. Miles was thirteen years older than me. We were poor company for each other. I knew you had that lovely house at Lucan, with the farm, but after you left it I lost track of you completely."

He told her about the leather business that his father had starved, so that when he died there was nothing left but debts, which Miles paid off by selling the house and land. He told her also about his silly mother who had so much wanted to keep it all that she had died soon after, accusing Miles to the last of having caused her death. He had been so shocked at her bitterness that he had gone into a sort of mental coma for several years. Even now, the memory of those years sickened him with their futility. He had been eighteen when his father died, and by the time he had begun to recover he was twenty-six. In the meantime, his younger sister, having failed to shake him out of his inertia, had emigrated to America, where she had married a Californian fruit-grower. Miles knew where she lived, but they had not written to each other for years. Perhaps he would see her again, now that things had changed so much. In the little silence that had fallen he said:

"My father was a strange man. Three of his five children died, and I think that he hardly noticed. I remember being brought into the drawing-room on my sixth birthday. He was

53

sitting by the fire, surrounded by books. He looked up irritably when I came near and said: 'And what is *your* name, my little man?' "

At nine o'clock Martin Doyle was shown in. He looked startled when he saw Germaine sitting by the fire. She answered him with a quizzical look, but made no comment. They spent a pleasant friendly hour there. Martin seemed no longer resentful, and he proved to be good company. It became clear that he was an enthusiast on the subject of balanced rations for pigs. He even went to the length of keeping two comfortable stout pigs in a pen behind the mill, where they lived like sultans on strange and various foods. His eyes sparkled with pride as he talked about them.

At ten o'clock Miles let his two guests out of the front door, and watched them down the avenue with feelings of intense satisfaction. He slept well for the first time since his arrival. It seemed that Sir Miles had failed in his promise to haunt the house.

The next morning Mrs. Hooper left early. Alice, the housemaid who served his breakfast, was seething with ill-concealed excitement as she put his coffee-pot on the table with a little crash. A drop splashed on to the cloth.

"Oh, glory be to God, Sir," she twittered. "Look at what I done to the clean cloth!"

"Never mind," said Miles patiently.

"It's me nerves, Sir. I'm shook, so I am. Did you know Mrs. Hooper was gone, Sir?"

He noticed that she was able to hold her nerves in check while she watched him for signs of shock. He liked Alice. She was young and plump and cheerful, and it said a great deal for Mrs. Hooper's strength of will that she had kept her so long in bondage. He said that he had known Mrs. Hooper was going, of course, and that Miss Germaine de Cogan would be living at the house from to-morrow.

"Blessed hour!" chanted Alice. "That I should live to see the day! Glory! Won't they all be charmed." She edged up to Miles's shoulder and almost nudged him. " 'Twas no harm to give the push to that old crow, with her whining and her pining. This will be a different house now, faith and soul it will!"

And she swept out of the room, almost airborne in her joy at being the bringer of such news.

Miles finished his breakfast happily. He had not expected Mrs. Hooper to leave so early, nor so quietly. Already the air of the house was lighter. That was partly Alice's doing. She had never dared to speak to him while Mrs. Hooper was in charge.

From that morning on, the house hummed with happy activity. Germaine came up from the lodge during the morning and Miles followed her about like a child. He went into the kitchen for the first time, and found a fat, comfortable cook waddling about. In the pantry next door, James had glasses and silver and a little boy to bully. Together with his cars, thought Miles, this must surely be all the heart of man could desire. There were vast linen presses, and an electric laundry. Germaine brought him to the dairy, and to the room next door where the eggs were weighed and measured and recorded in a little book. Portraits of hens hung on the walls, with comments written beneath. One hen was described as a typical non-producer: "Note the yellow colour of head, shanks and plumage, the hard, dried, scale-covered comb, the wrinkled ear-lobes and the full face."

"That exactly describes my Aunt Dilly, as I remember her," Miles commented.

Another hen, the author of a vast number of eggs, had a shiny, knowing eye cocked at the camera, a tremendous pendulous, red beard, and a juicy, meaty, fat comb.

"Hm. No better than she ought to be," said Miles.

He found that he owned incubators, and a wardress in a white coat tended his three hundred chickens. She showed him the miniature concentration camp in which they lived, and he quoted to himself:

The walls are hung with velvet that is black and
soft as sin,
And little dwarfs creep out of it, and little
dwarfs creep in.

He said something polite about the chickens, but he confided to Germaine afterwards that they gave him the horrors,
though no doubt they were very worthy little creatures.

In the library before lunch Miles thanked her for her conducted tour.

"I should never have had the nerve to do it alone," he said.

"Nonsense," said Germaine briskly. "You are not afraid of
anything. There was never a de Cogan born who was not convinced that he was mysteriously superior to everyone else."

"That is true," Miles admitted. "I suppose it was pride that
kept me from gambolling into the servants' quarters the day
after I arrived. I don't know at what stage our family pride
grew to such proportions," he went on. "I often think of our
ancestor, Miles de Cogan, who got a grant of land from Strong-
bow at Carrigaline. Perhaps it is all his fault. What did he look
like, I wonder? One would like to imagine him as an immense,
eagle-nosed giant, proudly glaring while his soldiers wiped out
the squalling natives and brought him the choicest maiden
blushing in a halter for a prize."

Germaine laughed.

"I think of him as a little fellow in a skirt of mail—or did
they wear skirts then? He would have looked rather silly, with
his toes turned down, in mail socks."

"One way or another, he founded a mighty family," said
Miles. "There are Cogans all around Carrigaline to this day.
I've been there, to see. But the weaker members who trickled off
to Dublin, and who had to be bolstered up with a preposition
—strangely enough, they are the proud ones. It is a crippling
disadvantage to be proud if you are poor. At least I found it so.
It was so difficult to work for anyone, especially at first. I was

like the unjust steward, when I began to earn my own living: to dig I was not able, to beg I was ashamed."

"And what did you do?" asked Germaine.

It was then that he told her about his Canning Street ladies, with their delicate kindnesses.

"They were very forbearing with me," he said. "I had been brought up to be a gentleman, and I was really fit for nothing else."

After lunch, Germaine asked him what he would like to do with the lodge.

"I had not thought of it at all," he said. "What do you suggest?"

"There are some people in the village who would be glad to have it," said Germaine. "Julia Hearn and her mother——"

"Of course!" Miles exclaimed. "They have that dead little house that I saw in the village. How soon can we ask them? Have they a telephone? It would be a wonderful thing to get them out of that place."

"Have you been in their house?" Germaine asked in surprise. "I had no idea that you would be so enthusiastic."

"There is no need to go into that house," said Miles. "It should be burned down. It's a little horror."

"Tom Reid wouldn't like to hear you say that," said Germaine. "He's very sensitive about his property."

"Then he should keep it in better order!"

"He has one or two other houses that are all right, but he seems to enjoy keeping Julia in discomfort. He could mend the roof, at least, and paint the outside, and put in a new window or two and some more plumbing——"

He hustled her off to offer the lodge to Julia, whom he had never seen, and then he sat there for a while reflecting happily on the pleasure of doing good deeds.

6

It was that same evening, after dinner, that he met Captain Merlin for the first time. There was a soft, blue stillness over the park, and Miles kept to the grassy margin of the avenue so as not to disturb the evening blackbirds. He recognized the Captain from Barne's description. It was an apt description as far as it concerned the extraordinary tweed suit, but Miles had not expected thin fair hair and penetrating blue eyes. He was a tall, lean man, and Miles noticed particularly his big knotted hands that kept on jerking ever so slightly. They were cruel, grasping hands. But for them he might have taken him for an ascetic. Captain Merlin greeted him in a high, querulous tone:

"You are Mr. de Cogan—Merlin is my name. I was just going to visit you."

They walked up the avenue towards the house. Miles said:

"I met your daughter a few days ago, at Reid's place."

Merlin shot him an uneasy sideways look.

"So you did. She told me. What did you think of her?"

Miles was startled at this question. If he were to answer it honestly, Merlin would get a shock, he thought.

"She's a charming girl," he said, and he thought that the other's smirk of pleasure was rather pathetic.

He wondered if it were simply over-concentration on the part of her father that had put Jane into the state in which Miles had seen her. But if this were so, it was the first time he had known affection to produce exactly that result. Then he remembered Merlin's cruel, twitching hands, and he was more convinced than ever that there was something ugly behind it all. Merlin was saying, as they stood on the doorstep:

"Fine place, Dangan House. I congratulate you on your inheritance. I knew Sir Miles well."

"I never met him at all," said Miles bluntly. "There was no one more surprised than I was that he made me his heir. The family was dying out, you see."

For some reason, a gleam came into Merlin's eye.

"You're not married?"

"Why, no," said Miles, pleased that there was someone who did not know all about him.

He brought the Captain into the library, and made him a large drink of whisky and water. Merlin walked over to the window with the glass in his hand.

"Your garden is looking well," he said. "My daughter is interested in gardening. Your man, Murphy, gives her slips and plants and so on, from time to time. I hope you won't mind if she comes along now and then, as she used to do?"

"I shall be delighted," said Miles.

This was the very thing for which he had hoped. If Jane could come to the house sometimes, perhaps Germaine would be able to help and advise her. He was surprised at Merlin for not being more jealous about her. She had had the appearance of a girl whose activities are closely guarded. He said that he would welcome Jane's advice about the garden.

"I'll send her up to-morrow," said the Captain, and looked meaningly at his empty glass.

As he poured him a second drink, Miles had a moment of doubt lest what he was planning were merely meddling. But so must Perseus have felt at sight of Andromeda: no doubt an inner voice had told him to let well alone and mind his own business. Miles felt that it would be quite unmanly of him not to free Jane Merlin from the rock to which she was chained, before the accounting sea-monster could swallow her up.

Presently he walked down the avenue with Merlin. It was almost dark now, with the blue velvet darkness of summer. They parted at the gate. As he watched the odd, tweedy figure ramble off, Miles wondered what it was that he had captained. Then he turned in at the lodge door.

He had not seen Germaine since she had left him to offer the lodge to Julia Hearn, and he was eager to know her answer. Sally led him, with a proprietary air now, into the front room. Germaine rose from a chair beside the fire and said:

"I brought Julia back with me. I hoped you would come in."

Julia Hearn was sitting on a low chair on the other side of the fireplace, and when Miles had been introduced she said:

"I can hardly believe that we are really going to live here."

For no reason that he could think of, Miles had imagined Julia as a tall, slender woman with a gently resigned expression. No doubt this vision grew partly from what he knew of her history. Germaine had told him that Julia had given up a promising career as a singer in order to look after her bad-tempered, domineering mother. Julia certainly was tall; when she stood up to shake hands with Miles, he had to look up into her face. Big women had always frightened him. She was big in every direction. And she had a huge mouth full of immense teeth, like tombstones. He almost felt that she might snap him up there and then, and crunch his bones. But she was not at all fierce, he soon discovered, but only sardonic. Her dark hair was long and smooth. He guessed her age to be about forty. He shuddered to think of her at eighty. Then he blamed himself for being so intolerant, and discovered that her voice, at least, had an attractive musical quality.

They planned that Germaine would move her things the next day, and that Julia would come to the lodge the day after that.

"Perhaps we will even be out of that house before the next shower of rain," she said.

They told him that quite a strong agitation had grown up among the people in the village against Reid's road-house. It was led by Paul Walsh, the owner of the hotel, who was supported by the doctor and the shop-keepers of the village. Miles had met Walsh, a dark-haired, dark-skinned young man whose father and grandfather had owned the hotel before him. It was easy to understand why he did not want a road-house in the village, for his customers were all quiet people who came for the fishing, the scenery or the good food and conversation of the hotel, and they would naturally resent such a noisy addition to their society. The doctor, whose name was Donovan, was a fisherman, too, and he feared that the roar of car engines would put the nerves of all the local fish on edge, so that they would move to quieter waters for the good of their health. His wife was urging him on to do something practical. She had been a nurse, and she talked about the beauties of Nature like the Children's Hour on the B.B.C., Germaine said. Father Dalton, the parish priest, did not want his simple parishioners' eyes opened to the possibilities of the sinful life, nor his more worldly parishioners furnished with nostalgic temptations.

"But what can they do to stop Reid?" asked Miles. "If he has bought and paid for the plot of ground, he can build a mosque on it, if he likes."

"I think you have never lived in a village until now?" said Germaine.

"Never," said Miles.

"Village people have plenty of time to spare," she explained, "and they never lose interest. If they really want to do it, they can force Reid to leave Dangan altogether."

"But how?" asked Miles, bewildered.

Germaine shrugged.

"By such a determined campaign that it would be bound to succeed. First they would study their man carefully, until they had found his most vulnerable point. Next they would start harrying him in small ways: anonymous letters, shouts in the night, small damage to his garden, a stone through a window. Then they might steal his dog, or force his housekeeper to leave. There would be pickets, of course, and notices painted on his walls. Then the shops would refuse to send him food, and the milkman would no longer call. And at last, when he would be thoroughly on edge, the trump card would be produced. At the end of a series of minor attacks, the attack on his weakest point whatever it is—would be enough to finish him. He would retreat in disorder, positively babbling."

Miles was almost babbling himself at the end of this recital. He saw that Julia was quite unmoved, leaning back against the cushions, watching him sardonically.

"But how do you know all this?" he stuttered. "Has it happened here, in Dangan, just like that?"

"Not yet," said Germaine. "I have known it to happen in other places, and the pattern is always the same. There is no reason to suppose that Dangan would be different. As soon as an agitation begins, it must work itself out. Usually the motive gets lost on the way."

Miles had to pause and collect his thoughts before he said:

"But what about the doctor? And Paul Walsh? These are educated people. They will be able to stop it before it goes too far."

Germaine shook her head.

"No. They won't be able to stop it. Within a very short time they will wish that they had not started it, but by then it will be too late. It will be out of control. You see, the village people would not start the persecution if they did not have support from some of their—leaders, I must call them. But once they have started it they will be reluctant to stop the fun, and private grievances will be remembered, and it will all be ugly and lopsided, and very different from the pure-souled agitation against a corrupting influence that it was in the beginning."

Miles looked helplessly from Germaine to Julia and back again.

"How do you know all this? Why are you so certain of it? Perhaps it won't happen like that at all."

"Perhaps not," said Germaine, but Julia said:

"Germaine is usually right in a forecast of that sort."

62

"How far have things gone?" Miles asked.

"There is a meeting outside the post office this evening," said Germaine. "It's probably going on now."

"Can't we go and intervene?" Miles jumped up. "I'm sure that if you told the people, as you have just told me, how it would all end, they would stop before it is too late."

Neither Julia nor Germaine moved. Germaine said cryptically:

" 'They have Moses and the prophets.' Anyway, no one would listen to women."

"They might listen to me," said Miles.

"I'm sorry I told you about it," said Germaine after a moment. "You can't do anything either. If you went down to the meeting and spoke, the people would either think that Reid had asked you to go, or else they would tell you kindly that you are not here long enough to understand their difficulties. There is only one way in which anyone can help, and that is by persuading Reid to give up his idea of having a road-house."

Miles, with his visual imagination, saw himself creeping like a snail unwillingly up Reid's drive, knocking at the door, making his little speech and then retreating hurriedly to the shrubbery pursued by a snarling Reid. He laughed aloud, and came to himself to find the two ladies watching him. Germaine said:

"That is exactly what would happen. If I were you, I would not waste any time in trying it."

"You see," said Julia to the astonished Miles. "She can see around corners."

So he agreed to become resigned to the ridiculous course of events. He was not at all of a practical turn of mind, and it was easy for him to become a detached and disapproving onlooker. Still, he experienced a sense of personal grievance because Dangan was not a fairy village after all, but a collection of houses full of very ordinary people.

" 'Wherever you go, yourself goes with you,' " he quoted to himself grimly from the sayings of the sententious old wiseacre who had been his nurse.

During the next week, Miles was only vaguely aware of the progress of the agitation against Reid. He found a complete list of his tenants among the papers that Barne had left in the library, and with his heart in his mouth he paid a visit to every one of them. He noticed that the first ones received him with surprise, indeed with suspicion, and they watched him for a while as if they were waiting for him to come to whatever unpleasant business had brought him. After the first evening, however, he found that he was expected, and he was ushered into the little kitchens with friendly, welcoming smiles. He had elected to pay these visits in the evenings, so that the men would be at home from work. At first they would stand silently by the fire while their wives did the talking, and the children peeped at him from the corners, with dark curious eyes like mice. Soon they would be asking him how he liked Dangan, telling him about its antiquities and the quality of the fishing, with the remote, dignified courtesy of countrymen. Only at the very end would they descend to discussing their own affairs. It hurt him to think how warily they talked then, as if they could not believe that he was really interested. In a number of houses he found an old man, a worker at the mill, living alone with his ageing wife. There had been no work for their children in the village, except as houseboys and handymen and gardeners to the neighbouring estates. It was not everyone that these occupations would suit, they said delicately.

Many of the houses were occupied by his own farm labourers, and rather to his surprise these looked quite prosperous. The reason was, as he presently learned, that in addition to the man's ordinary pay, each household received free milk and vegetables, and even a weekly ration of eggs. The excitement of a new idea had taken hold of him as he knocked at the door of the last house. It was opened by his steward, John Wall. He held the door wide and said, with a slightly quizzical smile:

"Come in, Mr. de Cogan. I heard you were making the rounds."

His house was a little bigger than the others. He led Miles into a tiny parlour, where the evening sun lay in gold bars on the linoleum, and a canary sang ecstatically in a cage in the window. The old man went across and put his finger into the cage, saying:

"Quiet now, Finn, so that we can hear our ears."

The canary perched on his finger, wiped his beak briskly on it twice, and fell silent. John shook him off gently and came back to ask Miles to sit down. There was a peaceful little pause for a moment and then Miles said:

"Yes, I have been making the rounds, and learning a number of things. My late cousin had some very enlightened ideas, but he didn't carry them far enough."

"He was one of the old stock," said Wall tolerantly. "It went against the grain with him to see a poor man with a bit of independence. He'd give the working men many a thing, but it had to be a gift, you see. Real feudal style."

Miles asked his next question tentatively, realizing the embarrassment that he might cause.

"Did the men like him?"

"They respected him," said Wall slowly, "but they didn't want to, if you understand me. He was always such a gentleman that it was hard to find anything against him. I got on with him very well myself, for he was a good man to the land, but he used to say that Sir Horace Plunkett was a damned radical." He shrugged. "I argued it out with him often enough, but the trouble was that his kind were all brought up to fear the working classes, and 'tis hard to get over the breeding. Just because my job was a tiny bit above an agricultural labourer's, he could talk to me, but there was always the gap between us that nothing could fill. He wanted to help the men, but as long as he had the old-fashioned ideas, he was only struggling and blundering."

"I wonder why he didn't develop the mill?" said Miles, impatient to start explaining his plan and still fearful that it would not be well received.

"He didn't want it to get too big," said Wall. "He liked everything to be in his own hands. He used to ride around the farm every morning and visit the men, and then go down to the mill afterwards. He was a man who found it very hard to delegate authority."

Miles wondered how his cousin would have felt if he had known how well his steward had summed up his character.

"Do you think the mill could be developed?" he asked.

"I could talk about that subject all night," said Wall.

They talked about it until midnight. It was almost pitch-dark before the old man got up and switched on the light, and Miles was secretly entertained by this old-fashioned economy. He learned that the flour and meal from Dangan Mills were not sold in the village at all, but exported to wholesalers in Dublin. The village shops got their flour from Kilkenny. There was no bakery in Dangan, and the bread came from Wicklow town. Martin Doyle had for years been frustrated in his desire to manufacture pig-meal, which was brought from a town in County Cork, over a hundred miles away. Wall agreed whole-heartedly with Miles that the whole economy of the village could be centred in the mill, bringing increased prosperity into every family, and considerably cutting down the emigration from the village. When Miles put forward his suggestion that the workers should each have a small share in the mill, the old man got up and solemnly reached for and shook his hand. Then he got out an exercise-book and they made notes of the points that they had discussed. They drew up a scheme which John Wall promised to explain at once to the people concerned. According to this scheme Miles was to retain one-tenth of the profits of the mill for himself, and Martin Doyle was to have one-tenth. The remainder of the shares was to be divided equally between the men permanently employed in the mill. Wall said he would discuss it all with Doyle, and together they would visit the shopkeepers in the village and urge them to buy the local products. The mill would start making Doyle's pig-food as soon as possible, and later they would start a small bakery. Miles said that he would write to Barne that very evening, so that he could prepare a draft agreement which they would all sign.

When Miles went home at last, he found that he no longer felt like an interloper as he let himself into the dimly lit hall. Now he clearly saw what was to be done, and, so far as he knew, none of the obstacles were insurmountable. If even one-half of the plans that were running through his head were to bear fruit, Dangan village would soon set a headline for every village in the country. He lay awake for a long time working out details and planning various courses of action. He knew that presently he would be pushed aside and the local people would take over the whole affair, and he was determined that he would not be disappointed at this. All he hoped for was to be pushed aside politely. By the time this would have happened he would have earned the right to live peacefully in Dangan House for the rest of his days.

Meanwhile the agitation against Reid had grown until, as Germaine had predicted, it became quite unmanageable. On Saturday evening, another meeting was held in the village. Standing on the edge of the crowd, Miles was disturbed to see all the eager faces about him, mouths half-open as if to help their twitching ears to take it all in. Dr. Donovan was making a speech from a kitchen table outside an open door. He was a middle-aged man, with a too-youthful expression. Miles squirmed for him, for he knew that the doctor had no idea that his words were being stored up, to be used later as proofs of holy writ. They would serve to back up every grievance in the parish, Germaine said, when he told her about the meeting later. She said the village people would interpret the doctor's speech as the signal to go ahead and persecute Reid to their hearts' content.

This was exactly what happened. Sunday was a day of rest, of course, and presumably the people's thoughts were on higher things. On Monday there was another meeting of protest against the road-house. Miles found James washing a car in the cobbled yard. James said that a decision on procedure was expected. He looked modestly down at his boots.

"I'm just back from there—I made a speech myself. And won't everyone be glad to have a poke at Mr. Reid," he said appreciatively. "This is a great day for Dangan, I'm telling you!"

"But this is very uncharitable," Miles protested. "How can you talk like that about a fellow man? Think of him at home now, worrying about all this. Don't you see that it's wrong——"

"Now, Sir, don't you be thinking about that at all," said James soothingly. "Mr. Reid has been riding for a fall for a long time. Would you believe it, Sir, when Sir Miles died, Mr. Reid thought that *he* was the big man in Dangan! There's nerve for you!"

Miles chuckled.

"Surely he had at least as good a right as I," he began, but James interrupted again:

"Excuse me, Sir. This is a thing that the likes of you could never understand, if I may say so. Just keep out of it. That's my advice to you."

He squeezed out the chamois with which he had been polishing the car windows, to indicate that the conversation was at an end.

"The proletariat takes over," thought Miles as he moved away.

He walked slowly along the back avenue hardly noticing where he was going. Just beyond the bridge he saw Dr. Donovan coming towards him, almost at a run. His head was down and his hair was disordered. It was not until he had almost collided with Miles that he noticed his presence. He started to pass, with a mumbled apology, but Miles laid a hand on his arm.

"What's the matter?" he asked bluntly.

Dr. Donovan stopped and looked at Miles with wide innocent eyes.

"I'm trespassing," he said. "Sorry."

"Oh, hang that!" said Miles. "What has happened down there?"

He waved in the direction of the village.

"It's my own fault," Donovan groaned. "I should have seen the gloating look in their eyes. They are having the time of their lives now, unctuously plotting revenge, in the name of Christianity, on that poor wretch."

"Reid?"

"Of course. They put me off the platform. And Paul Walsh, too. They said we would be better out of it. They said that we had helped to give them the idea and now we could leave the rest to them. Oh, if only I could give myself a good kick——!"

"Did you protest?"

"I protested until my hair stood on end, as you see." Signs of returning sense of humour, thought Miles. "I actually thought that they would push me off the platform by force, and I could not have that."

"Why not? You could have gone down fighting."

"But then it would have been harder for me to intervene later on. Don't you see?" he said impatiently at Miles's dubious expression. "They are determined to start something. They won't be cheated out of that. When they get over their first triumph I can get after them again with more chance of success."

"But why should they listen to you, then, either?"

"As long as the Irish climate remains as it is," said the doctor grimly, "they will have to listen to me. They know that I'll have them on toast when winter comes, with colds and influenza and bronchitis. I'll have the handle of a spoon down their throats, and they'll have to listen to me then, and no backchat either. In winter I'll be in and out of every house in Dangan. You'll see how my influence will be felt."

"I hope that Reid will survive until then," said Miles doubtfully.

"Oh, he's tough enough," said Donovan. He smiled suddenly at Miles. "I'm glad I ran into you. Talking about it has cleared my mind a little."

He turned on to the river bank.

"Where are you going now?" Miles asked.

"To say good night to the fish."

Miles watched him walk rapidly away, and then he went on more slowly towards the village.

When he arrived the meeting was just coming to an end. The street was full of excited people, the more intense because they were quite silent. The back of a lorry served as a platform this time, and Joe, the middle-aged pot-boy from the hotel, was finishing an impassioned speech.

"Men of Dangan," he declaimed, while the sweat poured down his face, "are you going to stand by and see our young people corrupted by this big Dublin slug? Are you going to let cars go cruising up and down the main street, and greasy tykes reaching in and whisking your wives and daughters away from the kitchen table?" There were one or two smiles at this vision. "You may laugh now," Joe thundered, "but wait till my words come true! Just wait until this respectable village is gone to the dogs, and then you'll be bleating that something should be done to stop it. Well, prevention is better than cure, I say!"

He went suddenly hoarse. The crowd burst into cheers. Joe took a tablet out of his waistcoat pocket and slipped it into his mouth. Then he said, in an almost conversational tone of voice:

"All right. You're on the side of morality and order. There's a few of us having a meeting below in my house to talk about what we'll do next, and we'll let you know what we decide."

He got down off the lorry and went through the open door of the cottage behind him. Miles watched thoughtfully while the crowd broke up into excited groups. He heard a word here and there of their conversation, and he noticed that the question of the road-house was hardly mentioned at all. Most of the talk seemed to concern Reid's high and mighty behaviour, and the expected pleasure of taking him down a peg or two. While he stood there, a man got into the lorry and drove it away. Miles was surprised to see that it was one of his own lorries and that the driver was Martin Doyle.

He walked through the village, and he noticed that he was greeted in a friendly way by everyone. It was uncomfortably obvious that he had been elected by the people to represent the anti-Reid spirit. No doubt this was because of the new co-operative scheme for the mill, which had been received with delight.

He let himself in through his front gate and walked along the drive through the dusk. A little more than half-way to the house he was surprised to hear a horse's hooves plunging about on the gravel before him. Then around the turn of the avenue came a huge black horse. One glance told him that the bad-tempered figure on its back was Reid. He was pulling savagely at the reins so that the horse side-stepped and pranced alarmingly. Miles stepped prudently on to the grass and re-marked to Reid that it was a fine night. Even as he said it he realized the appalling inadequacy of the remark. Reid had pulled the horse to a standstill and was sitting there, rock-like, blocking the avenue. It was rather like meeting the headless coach, Miles thought, as he watched the silent, venomous figure, and a prickle of physical fear ran down his spine. It was gone in a moment, and he said:

"It is Mr. Reid, isn't it? It's so dark I can hardly see properly——"

Reid laughed sourly.

"It's me all right. I've been calling on you—I'm warning you that you are on very shaky ground. I'm not a man that can be rough-handled."

"What on earth are you talking about? I never heard such nonsense! Who's rough-handling you?"

71

"You'll see," said Reid. "I won't take it lying down, by the way. You'll be hearing from me. Take my advice and don't be making yourself too comfortable here—it will be a nasty change for you if you do."

He kicked at the horse and it thundered off into the dark. Miles watched until it was out of sight.

"He should have given a devilish laugh," he thought. "What a perfect opportunity wasted!"

Still, he found that the incident worried him. He wondered what Reid had meant. Surely it was that Miles had no right to his inheritance, and that Reid was going to set about depriving him of it. Miles found that he was beginning to see the village point of view about Reid.

He spent the rest of the evening in the library with Germaine. He described the meeting in the village and his encounter with Dr. Donovan, but he could not bring himself to tell her about Reid's threats. It would have embarrassed him, and, besides, a whole philosophy had to be worked out now, so that he would be able to bear whatever was to come.

Before he went to bed, he wrote a letter to Barne, asking him to come down to Dangan as soon as possible. After some hesitation he described the agitation against Reid, and his own encounter with him in which Reid had seemed to cast serious doubts on his ownership of Dangan House. When he reached this point, Miles paused and read what he had written.

"That will show him that he must come at once," he thought.

He went out and posted the letter in the box by the gate, enjoying the walk in the peaceful night air.

Barne arrived the very next evening, at about six o'clock. Miles saw him drive up to the front door and hurried out to greet him. They went into the drawing-room where Miles had been sitting.

"I did not think you would have my letter so soon," he said. "It was good of you to come at once."

Before Barne could answer, the door burst open and James

shot into the room. His face was an ugly yellow, and he gulped and spluttered for half a minute, unable to speak. Miles had a glass of sherry in his hand, which he had poured for Barne. Now he walked across to the inarticulate and unpleasing James and thrust the glass into his hand.

"Here, man!" he said sharply. "Pull yourself together. Go on—tip her up and down she goes!"

James swallowed a mouthful of the sherry, and shivered.

"Now, what's up?" Miles asked abruptly. "Time for hysterics later."

"It's Mr. Reid, Sir," James whispered. "Mr. Reid. He's dead."

"When?"

"I don't know."

"At home?" James shook his head. "Where? Down in the village? An accident?"

Again James shook his head, and then he drew a long, shuddering breath.

"He's here, Sir, in the library. I—I found him just now when I went to do the fire. He's lying on the sofa, Sir. And he's dead."

"How do you know?" asked Barne. "Perhaps he's ill."

"Wait till you see him, Sir," said James. "Just wait till you see him!"

He turned suddenly and ran out of the room. Miles and Barne glanced at each other, and then by common consent they followed James out into the hall.

7

James was waiting for them at the library door. In the midst of his confused thoughts Miles found time to be thankful that the man had partly regained his self-control. He would never have expected James, with his somewhat blasé air, to be so upset at the idea of death. Anyone might have become excited or even frightened, but this unseemly hysteria was astonishing. In that moment before they went into the room, he wondered what had happened to Reid. A weak heart, perhaps, like so many big heavy men, combined with bad temper and unsuitably strenuous exercise. And why, oh why, had he chosen to die in Miles's library when he had a good home of his own? But that was an unworthy and an ungenerous thought.

James was beginning to twitter again.

"I can't open that door. Honest to God, I can't! Don't ask me to open that door!"

He backed away. Miles said soothingly:

"It's all right, James. I'll open the door."

He began to feel himself affected by James's fear. He seized the door-handle impatiently, twisted it, pushed the door open and marched into the room. Barne followed him. James, out in the hall, appeared to have burst into tears.

Miles stood for one long minute, while he took in the scene before him. Reid lay on the sofa, as James had said, and he was undoubtedly dead. From the bottom of his heart Miles pitied him, because now all his work and all his carefully built-up life had gone for nothing. There was hardly anyone to mourn for him, unless Barne would. Reid's parents were dead, he had heard, and he was not friendly with his only brother who still

74

carried on the blacksmith's business in Limerick. Barne could have the job of notifying the brother. Miles noticed now that Barne had backed out of the room again, probably shocked and upset at the manner of Reid's death. He wondered why Reid's limbs were twisted in that curious way. He had not known that people who died of heart attacks were so unpleasant to look upon. In fact, he had always understood that it was a rather peaceful sort of death.

He followed Barne out into the hall, and found him patting James on the shoulder and making frantically soothing noises. James was sitting with his head in his hands rocking to and fro and moaning like a Connemara woman over a dead turkey. Miles said sharply:

"Stop that at once!"

James stopped and looked up in surprise.

"That's better," said Miles. "Now there are several things to be done. Who let Mr. Reid in?"

"I don't know, Sir. Honest to God, I don't——"

"If you please, James," said Miles wearily, "try to behave normally. You make my head spin. Now go and find out when Reid got here, who let him in and what he said. And I want you to be about when the doctor comes."

"The doctor, Sir? And what would you want the doctor for? Isn't the decent man as dead as Finn MacCool?"

"It's the custom to call the doctor all the same," said Miles. "You get on with those things and leave the rest to me."

The only telephone was in the library. Miles encouraged Barne to go back to the drawing-room and pour himself a drink. Then he braced himself to reopen the door. Keeping his back turned towards the body, he lifted the receiver and asked the voice from the exchange to connect him with Dr. Donovan. While he waited, he reflected that Mrs. Hooper's sister, who operated the telephone exchange herself, would soon have an item of news calculated to send her shooting off her high stool as if it had suddenly grown red-hot. He knew that she always

75

listened to the conversations of her more distinguished customers. Presently he heard Dr. Donovan's voice say:

"Mr. de Cogan? Anything wrong?"

"Thomas Reid. Dead in my library. How soon can you be here?"

"Seven minutes."

That was all, but within four minutes every Dangan resident over the age of one year knew that Reid was dead. Curiously, the effect of the information on the village was not to bring excited groups of people into the street. Instead, they called their children in and shut their doors, and when Dr. Donovan drove through the village a few minutes later, the street was completely deserted. He was in too much of a hurry to notice this, or how the lace curtains in every window were fingered aside to let the occupants peer at him as he passed.

At Dangan House, he found Miles waiting on the steps. As he got out of the car, Donovan said:

"What's all this about Reid? Are you sure he's dead?"

"No doubt about it," said Miles. "Wait till you see him."

"But what happened to him? Reid was as strong as a bull."

Miles said tentatively:

"Perhaps he had a weak heart. I think that all this agitation against him in the village may have brought on a heart attack."

Donovan looked at him sharply.

"Let's have a look at him," he said. "I'll be amazed to find that he was so sensitive."

Miles led him through the door to the library. As they reached the door, James came hurrying from the direction of the kitchen.

"I've asked them all, Sir," he said, still in an excited, hysterical tone. "No one let him in. He must have come in by himself, so he must. No one knows anything at all about him or his doings."

"Here, what's the matter with *you*?" said Donovan to James. "What's all the excitement about? Now, you listen to me, Jim

76

MacDonagh. Don't you go making all the women have hysterics on me, or I'll take the hide off you. What have you been saying to them?"

Faintly, now, Miles heard shrieks of female fear from the service quarters. James looked over his shoulder a little desperately and said soothingly:

"Ah, now, doctor, sure I only told them that Mr. Reid was dead, all curled up like the worm of a poiteen still on the library sofa——"

"Did you say there is a curse on the house?" the doctor asked menacingly. "Did you say that this was the second corpse in a few months and that these things always go in threes? Did you say that this wouldn't happen in old Sir Miles's time, a fine decent gentleman? Did you leave those women shrieking for their mammies, and taking off their aprons, and reaching for their coats to go home? Did you? Did you?"

"Well, now, doctor——" James pleaded, but Donovan advanced on him threateningly and poked him in the chest with a long fore-finger.

"You get back in there, Jim, my boy, and take back every word of it. If I don't see them all busy cooking the dinner, or whatever they should be doing at this time of the day, when I go into the kitchen, I'll have your life. Go on, now, and be as smart about quietening them down as you were about stirring them up!"

James fled back to the kitchen, bleating promises of good behaviour. Donovan watched him go and then said with a satisfied snort:

"Well, that's that, I think. Now we can get on with the business in hand."

"That is not the first time you have quelled a revolution," said Miles gratefully as he opened the door.

Donovan stood up for a moment just inside the room. Then he went across and stood looking down at Reid, touched his hand for a moment and said:

77

"Yes, he's dead, all right. Poor fellow." He paused. "But that's no heart attack, you may take it from me."

"Then what is it?"

Donovan did not answer for a moment. Then he said:

"Have you touched him or moved him at all?"

"No."

"We'll have to call the police, you know. I can't give a death certificate. There will be an inquest." He glanced sideways at Miles. "This is a nasty business for you. Can you throw any light on it? Why should he choose to poison himself in your house?"

Miles shrugged helplessly. If Reid had come to the house and there deliberately poisoned himself, surely it could only be with some crazy idea of revenging himself for his fancied grievance against Miles. But he did not want to discuss this possibility with Donovan, who must by now be searching his own conscience on the subject of the meetings.

"I met Reid last night," said Miles cautiously, "and he seemed to have no intention then of committing suicide."

"You never know with a potential suicide," said Donovan. "Some of them seem to carry on quite normally—buy the next day's dinner, arrange to open the flower show next week—and then suddenly something snaps and they bump themselves off on the spur of the moment. On the other hand, others plan it all as carefully as a society wedding."

"I should have thought that Reid would have been the planning sort," said Miles. "Couldn't it have been an accident?"

"Oh, yes. Easily. Very hard to prove, though. Poor fellow. He could never bear me. It will be a relief not to have him about, though I know I shouldn't say it. He used to tell the local dowagers that I was no good at my job, but, fortunately for me, they regarded him as an upstart, and they wouldn't cock him up by taking his advice. Besides, they knew they had to have me on hand in case they went too far with trampling on their companion-helps or underfeeding their poor relations.

78

Poor old Reid. He scorned the commonalty and the County scorned him, so he fell between the two stools."

He fetched a long sigh. For all his expressed sympathy Miles thought that the doctor was almost exultant. It was very strange, even for a doctor, to stand in the dead man's presence and give off these opinions so smoothly. Donovan said:

"Well, now, we must summon the Guards."

He started towards the telephone.

"Which Guards?" Miles asked.

"In the village, of course. We have a sergeant and two privates to keep the peace in Dangan. They'll make a start, anyway, and if they want help I suppose they'll send to Dublin for someone."

With his hand on the telephone he paused and said:

"Perhaps it would be better not to give Miss Byrne too much information. I could drive down to the barracks and talk to them, if you would be able to stay here and make sure that no one comes in." Miles agreed to this and Donovan went on: "With your permission I'll visit your kitchen premises now and smooth down your staff with my well-known charm. I'll send James along to you and it would be well if you stayed here together until the Guards come."

Miles found the next half-hour very trying. After Donovan had gone, Barne emerged cautiously from the drawing-room. By silent agreement, Miles and James were standing in the hall by the open library door. Neither of them wanted to wait in the library in the unpleasing company of Reid. Barne looked white and frightened, but his eyes shone with what Miles supposed to be a legal excitement. In his customary suit of solemn dusty black, he looked, Miles thought, like a carrion crow trying to restrain his instincts in the presence of more fastidious birds.

"His first task", thought Miles grimly, "can be to protect me from the effects of Reid's choice of a place to die."

"What did Donovan say?" asked Barne eagerly as he padded down the hall. "Will there have to be an inquest?"

"Donovan says that Reid was poisoned," said Miles bluntly.

"Good gracious! Poisoned! Surely he had a heart attack."

"Donovan says not."

"Probably Donovan doesn't know what he is talking about," said Barne pettishly. "He spends more time fishing than practising medicine."

"Excuse me, Sir," said James in a very subdued tone. "I know something about heart attacks myself, and I never saw one that looked like Mr. Reid. Never."

"What do you know about heart attacks?" asked Miles.

"Well, Sir, the grandmother died of a heart attack, and a couple of the aunts. A neighbour or two was took off in the same way, and somehow it happened that I got a good look at them all. They didn't look one bit like Mr. Reid. I'll take me oath on that."

"Some other natural cause, then," said Barne impatiently. "A diabetic coma, a stroke—anything at all."

"Donovan says that he was poisoned," said Miles. "No doubt he will take steps to find out how. He's gone for the police. He said that that was the first thing to be done."

"He's quite right, of course," said Barne, "but I don't like it."

"I can't say I like it much myself," said Miles dryly.

Now that Barne was there, he felt at liberty to send James in search of Germaine. He thought that she might be visiting Julia Hearn at the lodge. James, very glad to be released, panted off to find her. When he had gone, Miles remembered that he had not told Barne about his new arrangement with Germaine. He did so now, glad of a diversion of any sort. Barne received the news without much apparent interest.

"I should have waited for a while, if I were you," he commented. "I hope you won't regret it."

"Mrs. Hooper didn't like to be asked to go," said Miles. "But she'll get another job."

"It suited her to work near her sister, I suppose," said Barne.

"Still, she needn't have got into such a state about it. She must have known that you would make changes."

They were silent after that. Miles felt suddenly exhausted, and the prospect of the uneasy days before him made his head ache. It was a relief when they heard Donovan's old car thundering on the gravel again. A moment later the hall was full of people.

8

"I brought the whole force with me," said Donovan proudly. "We locked the door of the barracks."

He introduced Sergeant Lawlor and his two henchmen, Carr and O'Shea. They were all in uniform. The sergeant was a big, heavy, grizzled man with a slow humorous eye and a slow, gentle voice. Carr, for all that he measured up to the required standard in height, had the teeth and hair of a red squirrel, as well as the helpless, drooping hands. He had round, brown, beady eyes, full of a squirrelly surprise. O'Shea had obviously been convinced at an early age that concentration was the way to success. He took in everything with a penetrating eye, rendered all the more fierce by the heavy blackness of his hair and eyebrows. They were both younger than the sergeant. All three had removed their uniform caps when they came into the hall. Miles thought, as he always did, how oddly bare a policeman's head looks without a cap.

A fourth man had been standing quietly just inside the door while Miles acknowledged the introductions. He was in plain clothes, but his square shoulders and straight back helped Miles to guess at his occupation before Donovan led him forward and introduced him as Inspector Henley from Wexford.

"He's staying at the hotel," he said, looking at his capture with delight. "He's on his holidays, fishing. I had met him before, so when I saw him walking down the street, I just stopped and made him get in, and brought him along."

"This is not a holiday for you," said Miles as he shook hands.

"I'm very glad to be able to help," said Henley quietly.

82

Immediately Miles felt as if a burden had been lifted from him. It was difficult to say in what way Henley inspired this confidence. At first sight he should not have been impressive. He was smaller and slighter than the others, and his fair hair was beginning to recede a little from his high forehead. He had the deep grey eyes and the quiet hands of an intellectual, and though his expression was serious and sympathetic now, it was possible to observe an underlying humour sprung from complete unselfishness. At this point in his reflections Miles cautioned himself against falling into the trap of wishful thinking. Still, he found that he was no longer afraid, and he led them into the library without any further delay.

They crowded in the doorway and stared like laymen for one long moment. Then Lawlor broke the spell by moving forward, saying:

"The poor man. There's an end I wouldn't wish to anyone."

And there's another man who did not like Reid, thought Miles in surprise. Lawlor had been unable to keep the note of satisfaction out of his voice. Now he became irritated with Barne who was twittering at his elbow, pulling his sleeve and saying in a querulous tone:

"Surely we don't all have to be here? I don't see why we should all have to stay and watch this."

"Of course not." Inspector Henley stepped forward and took Barne by the arm. He nodded to Lawlor. "You go ahead and measure everything, and you can come and find us later. Would you like to stay, Donovan?"

"I'll stay," said the doctor. He cocked an eye at Miles. "Have you had dinner yet?"

Startled, Miles realized that he had not. He looked at the hall clock and found that it was only a quarter-past seven. He solemnly invited Donovan to dinner, with the remark that it was likely to be late. The local Guards refused his offer of food, but Henley accepted it. There and then he telephoned to the hotel to say that he would not be back for dinner, and at last they came out into the hall again. As he shut the door, Miles noticed that Lawlor was setting about his strange routine as confidently as if he were accustomed to stowing away the remains of bold bad barons every day of the week.

Back in the drawing-room he made his guests sit down and poured them a drink each. As he settled with his own glass in an armchair in front of the fire he seemed to catch the eye of his ancestor over the mantel. There was a smug look about that old Sir Miles this evening, as if he were pleased that there was a violent death about the place again—quite like old times.

Barne was saying:

"I don't like it. I don't like it one bit. I thought he would just be taken away quietly. Mrs. Barne won't like it either. Those Guards all over the place. All the publicity——"

"Now, please don't worry," said Henley soothingly. "They will be very careful. They understand quite well about the publicity."

Barne grumbled into his drink and seemed dissatisfied. Miles wondered what he had to complain of. Surely the injured party was Miles himself, if anyone, with a stout, belligerent ghost now permanently blighting the library, a room of which he had grown very fond. He would not have expected Barne to be so easily upset. Perhaps he was mostly afraid of Mrs. Barne, as usual.

Inspector Henley was quietly studying both of them, and wondering how soon he would be able to detach Barne from Miles. He had heard about Reid and his road-house, and the protest meetings, within an hour of his arrival at the hotel that morning. On former visits to Dangan he had met Reid alive, so that he knew what he had been like in character. For his own good reasons, Henley was already planning to persuade the authorities to let him cancel his holiday and probe the reason of Reid's death himself. He had good hopes that he would succeed in this, for his superiors could always be relied on to make intelligent use of such circumstances as his knowledge of the village and its inhabitants. Already his professional habit of mental note-taking had told him one or two things. For example, he knew that Miles did not believe that Reid had committed suicide, though it would have been such a neat, convenient solution.

He was on the point of asking Miles bluntly if he could speak to him in private when Barne tossed off the remainder of the drink and stood up.

"I'll go up to my room, I think," he said. "You should do the same. This is our last quiet moment for the rest of the evening."

He stumped out. Henley leaned forward and said in a low voice:

"I've been waiting to talk to you alone, Mr. de Cogan. Do you know who I am?"

Miles looked at him in bewilderment.

"I'm not very clever this evening," he apologized. "Body in the library, you know. Have we met?"

"You know my mother," said Henley, gently. "She has a shop in Canning Street."

"You are Pat!" Miles was on his feet in an instant, wringing the Inspector's hand. " 'My son in the Guards!' Why, I know all about you—the marks you got in your examinations, the number of infectious diseases you have had—you're not a bit like your mother," he finished.

"I'm told that I take after my father," said Pat.

"I remember him," said Miles vaguely. "He was at the party. I wish you had been there. It was a great party."

"I was out of town. I'm stationed in County Wexford, you know."

"What sent you to Dangan?" said Miles. "You're just in time to hold my hand."

Pat explained that he had often spent fishing holidays in Dangan. He was thinking how pleased his mother would be that he was able to help her pet out of this difficulty.

It was early yet to decide whether Reid had been murdered, but the possibility had to be taken into account from the beginning.

He watched Miles for a moment before he went on:

"What do you think happened to Reid?"

Miles was standing up to all this very well, Pat thought. He appeared to have a habit of self-control which was supporting him now. Many a man would be having a fit of hysterics, excusing himself on the ground that it is good to let off steam. Pat thought that Miles would be impatient of such indulgences. He seemed to be philosopher enough to know that they would only make his role more difficult. Whatever the reason for his air of half-humorous resignation, Pat was grateful for it because it made his own task easier. Meditatively Miles answered his question:

"Donovan says that he was poisoned."

"Yes, he said so as we came here in his car."

"But Barne says that Donovan doesn't know his job, and that Reid died naturally."

"We'll soon establish whether that happened or not," said Henley. "What do you think about it yourself?"

"I don't know," said Miles slowly. "I didn't know Reid very well, of course, since I've only lived here for the last few weeks. But I should say that he was one of those people who imagine that death could have no possible connection with themselves. You get it even in quite religious people. It's not that they think they are immortal, or that a special exception will be made for them; it's almost as if they don't *believe* in death. It's a difficult thing to express. I thought that was how Reid's mind worked. I can't imagine him committing suicide without weeks of frightened hysteria first, and without a very good reason indeed—probably a financial reason. I don't think that any personal reason would be sufficiently powerful."

"We can find out about his financial state," said Pat. "So you think he was murdered?"

"I didn't say that," said Miles in alarm.

"You left no other possibility, did you?"

"An accident."

Pat shrugged.

"Adults rarely take poison by accident. Still, we must go into that question too."

He explained that it would take a day or two officially to establish himself in charge of the investigations, but that he thought he would be allowed to start on his inquiries at once.

"In that case, you should come and stay here," said Miles eagerly. "I have at least ten spare bedrooms," he went on as Pat hesitated, "and you will be no trouble."

"But you will not be able to forget about this business for one moment, if I am in the house."

"Don't let that stop you from coming," said Miles grimly. "I won't be able to forget about it anyway. In fact, it would be a comfort to me to know something of the progress of your investigations. To be quite in the dark would be maddening. Please come," he said appealingly. "I'll even give you the library all to yourself to work in. I'm not likely to want to sit there myself for some time."

"Very well," said Pat after a moment's thought. "I'll have to arrange it with the authorities, but I don't think they will make any objection."

He was thinking what a peaceful place this house would be to work in—even for such unacademic work as his own. Down at the hotel there would be curious spectators every time he went in and out, and quiet little men in tweed caps appearing mysteriously at his elbow pressing drinks on him and trying to pump information out of him. In the interval between the news of Reid's death reaching the village and the arrival back of Donovan for the Guards, Henley had had time to notice the village people's reaction. He had thought it very curious. There had been a positively guilty air about the way in which they all

87

had quietly gone indoors avoiding each other's eyes and hardly speaking at all. It had been so marked that he had noticed it, standing at his bedroom window overlooking the street, long before he knew the reason of it. Down in the bar, Joe had grudgingly told him the news and had then scuttled out of the bar, leaving him to finish his drink alone. This from Joe was unprecedented.

There were things going on at Dangan House, too, that Pat felt he would like to observe. If he were staying at the house, information would reach him almost unnoticed. And he could walk down to the hotel at any time he liked.

"There is one thing I should like to ask you before that little solicitor comes back," he said. "Why is he in such a state of excitement about this? In his profession, surely he must have seen a few nasty things before this?"

"Barne was a friend of Reid's," said Miles. "A friend and an admirer too. Reid must have had very few friends. Barne got on well with him, and thought a lot of his business ability, I think. He was very anxious that Reid and I should be friends, but that's not likely now." Miles stopped suddenly. "I must give up saying that sort of thing," he said apologetically. "It gives the wrong impression. I'm really very distressed about Reid's death, believe me."

"Of course. Don't try to put on an act for me. I understand you very well," said Henley.

And he really does, thought Miles, and breathed easier.

"Why is Barne here now?" Henley asked.

"I sent for him to talk about business," said Miles.

He did not feel ready to give any more details until he had time to think it over alone. It had already occurred to him that it might not be necessary to reveal the silly things that Reid had said to him on the evening before his death. A word of warning would silence Barne. Henley was saying:

"Could I have a word with your man, James? He knows me. We met in the village when I was here before."

"He's gone to look for my cousin, Miss de Cogan," said Miles, looking around vaguely. "If you will excuse me, I'll go myself and see if he has come back yet. I think this is not an evening for ringing bells."

Left alone, Inspector Henley relaxed in his chair and looked into the fire. How well Miles fitted in here, he thought. It was obvious that he had lived this sort of life before now, perhaps in his youth. Otherwise he would have looked more surprised, or more smug, or more awkward. And his years of poverty seemed to have left no mark on him. No one would have guessed that only a few weeks ago he had been eking out a miserable living by making up the accounts of small shops. Henley had said that he understood Miles quite well, but this was far from the truth. There was a depth and a remoteness about him that Henley felt would not be easy to penetrate. Miles had lived alone so much that he had a self-sufficient air about him. Talking to him about personal things produced a feeling of embarrassment in Henley, as if he were trying to probe into the private lives of a married couple. Miles was like a man married to himself.

When James arrived a few minutes later, Pat felt that he was much easier meat. James had come in looking frightened but belligerent. When he saw Pat he leaped across the room and pawed his shoulder, while Pat tried to struggle to his feet.

"Well, Mr. Henley, you're a sight for sore eyes, so you are," he babbled. "I came in here thinking to be grilled and gruelled and ground by some big lump of a peeler from Dublin, and I can tell you truly that it is a great relief to find 'tis only yourself. Lord, sir, there's terrible doings here. Terrible doings, and no mistake. Enough to frighten an honest man."

"Sit down, Jim," said Henley. "There is no need to be frightened."

James sat on the edge of a chair, squeezing his hands nervously together, the perfect picture of a man with a guilty conscience. Pat watched him for a moment and then said gently:

"Why should you be so worried because poor Reid killed himself?"

"Oho, no. Mr. Reid didn't kill himself," said James confidently. "Whoever told you that is a liar, sir, you may take it from me. I'm surprised at you for being such an innocent, so I am."

"Do you know something about it then? How are you so sure he didn't kill himself?"

"Because he was too fond of himself, that's why. He wouldn't have hurt a hair of himself, let alone swallow a dose of poison that would curl him up the way he is."

"Perhaps he didn't know it would have that effect."

"Maybe not," said James doubtfully. "But he was a terrible man for taking precautions and working things out and buying little books about how to do everything."

"Well, then, what do you think happened to him?" asked Pat.

He was interested to see how Miles's and James's estimates of Reid's character tallied. Of course, the explanation could be that they had discussed it already. James was looking frightened again, and his closely cut hair seemed to pop up on his head.

"I don't know, sir," he said, "and that is the truth. But you'll be hearing about me, for certain sure, and I want to tell you my side of the story first."

"That's a sound idea," said Pat. "Don't be afraid of me. If you didn't kill Reid yourself you have nothing to fear."

But this speech, which he had meant to be soothing, nearly sent James into hysterics again.

"That's it, sir," he chattered. "That's the trouble, that's what I'm afraid of. Oh, that's what's killing me altogether——"

"Stop! Take a deep breath," said Pat sharply. "Now, speak slowly and keep your hair on. I won't eat you."

James gulped and then seemed to take hold of himself.

"It's all about a fighting speech I made the other night," he said. "We had the back of a lorry for a platform, and it was a grand fine evening and everyone came out to listen. Man, 'twas like old times, and I got carried away. 'There was blood spilled in Dangan before,' I said, 'and maybe there will be again.' I was talking about the crossness", he explained delicately, "when we ambushed the Crosseley tender full of Black and Tans below at the cutting——"

"But you couldn't have been there then," said Pat incredulously. "That's more than thirty years ago."

"I was eight years of age," said James defiantly. "I used to hear them talking about it every night afterwards while I was a young lad, and I used be heart sorry it was all over before I came up."

He contemplated this grievance for a moment while Pat covered up an inward chuckle. Then he went on:

"So you see, I was thinking of that, and maybe I incited someone to do in Mr. Reid. The people were terrible cross that evening, and when I said 'Blood' they all shouted like they was mad for a sup that very minute. I'm thinking now that maybe someone came away from the meeting and put something in Mr. Reid's way so that he drank it, and I'm to blame."

"But there's no blood on Reid," Pat consoled him.

"That's so," said James disconsolately. "But that's only what you might call a technicality."

Although he did not want to show it, Pat feared that this might be the explanation of Reid's death. A simple, suggestible person in the village might conceivably have poisoned Reid in the belief that he was doing a public service. He cautioned James not to speak of his fears to anyone. Then he went on to ask who had let Reid into Dangan House, and the hour of his arrival. He heard for the first time that no one had let him in.

"But are you sure? Did you ask everyone?"

James nodded eagerly.

"I asked them all, every one. No one let him in. No one saw him at all. And indeed it was like his brazen ways to walk in without knocking."

"Ssh," said Pat. "The man is dead."

"God rest him," said James automatically.

"Whose business would it be to let him in?" asked Pat.

"Mine, if I was in the house. Alice, if it was the morning, and Jenny, if it was after lunch. But none of them saw hair or hide of him."

"I'll see them myself later on," said Pat, and with further warnings he got James outside.

He was making notes of the conversation when Lawlor's head appeared around the door.

"Ah, here you are, sir," he said. He came across to the fire-place and stood warming his huge hands and looking into the blaze. "The evenings are still cool. What do you make of this?"

"Too many people will be glad that Reid is out of the way," said Henley. "You should know all about their reasons."

"I know a good many of them," said Lawlor. "I won't miss him much myself, though I had better not say that to anyone but yourself."

"What had he done to you?" Pat asked curiously.

"Oh, nothing very serious," said Lawlor, but Pat noticed that he flushed a little at the recollection. "Mr. Reid could never understand the kind of person who is content to go on doing his job from day to day as best he can, not making customs and not breaking customs, as we say in Gaelic. He thought that I should be progressive like himself, and he got real mad when I said that if the whole nation got on and became accountants there would be no one to keep the peace. He wrote to Dublin about me, with some imaginary complaint." Lawlor shrugged. "They told him politely to go and have a run for himself, so there was no harm done, but I didn't like it all the same."

"No wonder." Pat contemplated this story for a moment. "Does anyone know this?"

"Carr and O'Shea have wind of something, but they knew Reid so well that they took no notice. I asked Mr. Barne about it once when he was up here to see the old man. I met him outside the hotel, where he always used to go for a drink before coming up here. He said that I could sue Reid if I wanted to, but that it would be foolish to do that because the whole thing would get too much publicity."

"That was good advice. Had you thought of suing Reid?"

"Of course not. It would have been madness. Being a lawyer I suppose Mr. Barne's mind would run on actions. He probably thought I'd think of it myself, and wanted to put me off from the start. Anyhow, I couldn't finance an action like that out of my few pounds a week. So I said no more about it."

"And Reid?"

"He was sure he had me in the soup," said Lawlor. "He was very cocky for a few days, and then all at once he began to look punctured, and he began to keep out of my way. The cousin in the office in Dublin had told me all about it, of course, so I knew the answer he was getting a couple of days before he got it."

"That was nice," said Pat. "A great advantage of living in a small country is that there is always a cousin in the office."

"It can have its drawbacks too," said Lawlor with feeling.

They spent the next half-hour arranging for the disposal of Reid. Lawlor left Carr in charge of the library.

"Carr is terrible," he explained to Henley, "but he'll do a little job like that all right."

They arranged to meet in the morning, by which time they hoped that the immediate cause of Reid's death would have been discovered.

9

Dinner was less embarrassing than Henley had expected. Donovan was a great help, for he kept up a flow of talk about fishing and farming and the peculiarities of his elderly patients. Barne was irritably silent and he looked with dislike at his food. Jenny, the parlourmaid, served the meal, on Miles's suggestion. She was willowy and disdainful, and Pat was relieved that it was not the semi-hysterical James who had charge of his soup plate. Jenny looked incapable of spilling soup down anyone's neck. Miles was an attentive host, but a tightness at the corners of his usually humorous mouth showed the strain that was upon him. Germaine, in a black dress, sat at the other end of the table from Miles, and chatted firmly with Donovan. Pat liked her, though she too had the disconcerting remoteness that he had noticed in Miles. The meal was a good one, in spite of the excitements of the evening. It rather surprised Pat that there were still people in Ireland who could afford to live in such old-fashioned style. He supposed that it was the income from the mill and the estate that made it all possible—this delightful mixture of landed gentleman and honourable business man. It had been the choice of the old man to live like this, presumably because he had been brought up to it, and Miles seemed to have made very few changes.

He noticed that there was no family resemblance between Germaine and Miles, unless it was an appearance of habitual good humour.

They had coffee in the drawing-room from old Crown Derby cups. Barne drank his, black and unsweetened like himself, and then said:

"I'm going to bed."

He stumped out of the room. Germaine looked after him with raised eyebrows before turning to apologize to the others for his rudeness.

"He's very upset and nervous to-night," she said. "We must give him the privilege of an old family friend."

"I've just realized that not one of us said that we were sorry Reid is dead," said Miles. "Barne must have thought it very strange. It's no wonder he doesn't want to sit with us for the evening."

"I never could understand what he saw in Reid," said Germaine thoughtfully.

"These things are often inexplicable," said Donovan. "I wonder what the County will think of this business of Reid dying in your house."

"They'll be calling," said Germaine grimly. "Alice's sister is parlourmaid at Mrs. O'Kelly-Brennan's, for a start, and she won't leave anyone in the dark, you may be sure. I'll receive them myself, Miles, in here."

"Thank you," said Miles in heartfelt tones. "That is very kind of you. I should never know what way to take them. Officially, I suppose, they will come to sympathize with us."

"Yes," said Germaine. "And I'll steer the conversation around to Mrs. O'Kelly-Brennan's brother who was in gaol for forgery, and Mrs. Jeremy-Smyth's daughter who brought home a shameful bundle, and Mrs. Wilmott's husband who climbed a holly tree and said that he was Mad Sweeney, which was regrettably like the truth. I'll remind them how much neighbourly sympathy means on these distressing occasions, and I hope that the first batch to come will warn off the others."

"But are these your friends?" asked Pat tentatively.

"Certainly," said Germaine, "but we understand each other."

After a while, Pat excused himself, saying that he would walk down to the hotel for his suitcase. He declined with a shudder Miles's offer of James to drive him. Donovan made no move to go. Henley visited the library, where Carr was fiercely guarding the now-vacant sofa and encouraged him to redouble his vigilance. As he passed the drawing-room door on his way out of the house he heard an eager hum of voices within.

The walk to the village was pleasant. The night air was cool and scented, and he chose to go by the front avenue because it was the longer way. At a place where the avenue took a turn, he thought he heard a rustle of grass on the high field above him. He stopped and listened. It was probably a cow, he thought. Still he called softly:

"Who is there?"

There was no reply, but there was no mistaking the sound of hurriedly retreating footsteps. He made no attempt to follow, but continued thoughtfully on his way to the village.

At the hotel he found Paul Walsh in the hall. Since there was no one else in sight, Pat told him at once about Miles's invitation to stay at Dangan House.

"You've heard about Reid, of course," he added.

"Yes, poor fellow. Who would have thought it would end like this?"

Here was still another man whose problems were solved by Reid's death, thought Pat. As an old visitor to Dangan, he had no doubt of the reality of the threat to Walsh's business that Reid's road-house would have been. He said that he hoped to be allowed to conduct the inquiry into the manner of Reid's death.

"There will have to be an inquest, I suppose," said Walsh with distaste. "Could his doctor not be found and asked to certify that he had a bad heart, or whatever he had——"

"He died of poison, we think," said Pat carefully.

There was silence for a moment. Walsh's face went blank. Then he said vaguely:

"How—how short-sighted of him. There was no need to do that."

"There is some doubt as to whether it is suicide," said Pat.

Walsh gave him a long stare and then said:

"I think I need a drink. Will you join me?"

Pat agreed. He knew that Walsh had made a rule never to drink in his own bar, but this was surely an occasion for making an exception. They went into the bar together. It was a pleasant room, panelled and leathery, with comfortable semicircular corner seats. On one of these they saw Joe, leaning back against the cushions, his head resting against the wall, his eyes shut and his mouth regrettably open. Otherwise the room was empty.

Walsh darted across and laid his hand on Joe's shoulder. Joe stirred and sagged stupidly, but his eyes opened, staring into his employer's face. He got up unsteadily, with a tremendous effort, and grinned weakly.

"What's the matter with you?" asked Walsh sharply.

"Must have fallen asleep, sir," Joe stammered apologetically. "I never closed an eye all night last night."

"Why not? Are you ill?"

"No, no, sir." Joe's speech was not thick, but his eyes had a slightly glazed look. "There's nothing the matter with me."

He walked firmly enough around behind the bar. Walsh looked at him in a puzzled way and Pat could see that he was trying to make up his mind whether Joe had committed the final crime of a barman, that of getting drunk. Pat had seen people in Joe's condition before, and he knew that he was not drunk.

"I just sat down for a minute," said Joe, talking very fast. "I must have dropped off to sleep. I don't know what came over me. It looks bad before the customers, but by the mercy of God there warn't no customers there."

He was fumbling under the counter, and now he took out his little pill-box. Although he held it out of sight below the counter level, Pat knew what he was doing. He reached a long arm in over the counter and closed his hand over the little box. Joe turned his head slightly and quickly flipped the tablet that

97

he had abstracted into his mouth. Then he turned to stare at Henley. Walsh was staring too. Joe said, in a dead voice that trailed away at the end:

"Well, gentlemen, what'll you have?"

"Where did you get these?" asked Pat softly.

There was no need for the question, because a chemist's label was stuck on the little box. It said: "J. Ross, Chemist, Dangan." Joe licked his lips and his eyes flew to the label. He said sullenly:

"There's Johnny Ross's name on the box as plain as a pikestaff."

"Did he give them to you?"

"Yes."

"What are they?"

"Benzedrine. To keep me awake," he burst out savagely. "What's all the fuss about? A fellow has to have something to keep him awake, doesn't he?"

He appeared to see no incongruity in the fact that he had just complained of being awake all night. It seemed that his pills were only too effective.

"How long have you been taking them?"

"Maybe a year. Maybe not so much." Suddenly he snatched at the box. "Give me that! It's mine."

Pat held the box out of reach. He saw Paul Walsh looking from one to the other of them in amazement. Pat said quietly:

"Did everyone know that you kept them under the counter here?"

"How should I know? I didn't show them to anyone. There's no sin in taking a few little pills to keep me awake, is there? People take pills for everything nowadays, don't they?"

"Did you always keep them in the drawer?" Pat insisted.

"Sometimes they were in the drawer and sometimes they were in my pants pocket."

"Are there any of them missing? Look in the box, and see."

He took off the lid so that Joe could see the contents of the box, while he still held it out of reach. Joe scowled at it.

"I don't know," he said at last. "I thought there was more than that. But I don't know. What's all the questions for? You give me back my box. I'll see a solicitor, so I will. I'll get Mr. Barne after you. I'll get back my property——"

"Joe," said Walsh sharply. "What's come over you? I never heard you speak like that to a customer before."

"He's not a customer," said Joe contemptuously. "He's a damned snooping policeman."

"Have you heard that Mr. Reid is dead?" Pat asked.

Joe turned his back and said between his teeth:

"Sure, all the world heard that. And no loss, the big greasy bosthoon, the dirty, crawling, mangy——"

"Hold on," said Walsh. "The man is dead."

"I'm saying 'Good riddance'," said Joe venomously.

"I think he was poisoned with some of your pills," said Pat.

There was a little silence while Joe stared, pop-eyed. Then he said hoarsely:

"Did you say with my pills? Are you making out that I gave them to him?"

"I didn't say that," said Pat.

"No, but you meant it. Because I told him to keep away from Nora. Because I told him not to be putting ideas into her head, making her want to leave her daddy and go working first in his new pub, where the Dublin jackeens would be glauming her, and after that to Dublin where she'd maybe go to the bad altogether on me and I'd never see her again. I told Mr. Reid to keep away from her. I told him what I'd do to him if he wouldn't let her alone. Maybe if I got the chance I'd have poisoned him too." Suddenly his rage was spent. "But sure, I never got the chance, and now I needn't bother."

He fell silent. After a moment Walsh said shakily:

"Two brandies, please, Joe. That suit you, Henley?"

"I'll have a Guinness," said Pat mildly. "Let's have them in your office, shall we?"

A tweedy fisherman, studded with flies, bubbling with hearty sportsmanship, had just come in, and was lifting himself on to a high stool at the bar. They carried their drinks into Walsh's little office next door. Walsh drank some of his brandy thirstily and then put the glass on a small table by the fire.

"I needed that," he said.

Pat took a meditative drink of his Guinness and said:

"Now tell me all about Joe. Do you know what he was talking about?"

"Oh, I know what he was talking about, all right," said Walsh wearily.

In the next few minutes Pat watched him with interest. He had never taken much notice of Walsh before, except to observe that his hotel had a pleasant atmosphere. In spite of his profession, Pat was a shy man, and he had not pressed himself on Walsh, who often had a busy, preoccupied air. His heavy black hair, square jaw and autocratic eye had rather frightened Pat, but now he observed that as with many another tall, handsome young man, God had not thought it necessary to do him well in brains. He had the concentrated earnest frown of a man who fears to overwork his brain, but who admits that it must be a fine thing to be clever. Pat thought, too, that life had given Walsh several unpleasant surprises, and that the effect had been a slightly souring one.

"Joe lives in the village, here. Has done all his life. His father was a labourer at the mill."

"What is his other name?" asked Pat, who had got his notebook and pencil out.

"Joe Connolly. His wife is dead, and he has this one daughter, Nora, a forward, noisy little piece of about sixteen. But Joe thinks the world of her. His blood boils at the thought of a threat to her virtue, or even a suggestion that way. She rather invites comment of this sort, because of her screeching ways, but Joe thinks of her as a shy Irish maiden. He had a row with Reid about her, because Reid said he would give her a job in this road-house of his."

"So that's what Joe was referring to just now?" asked Pat.

"Yes, that was it. They live a few doors down the street, in one of de Cogan's houses, as a matter of fact."

Pat still had Joe's pill-box in his hand. He threw it into the air and caught it again, so that the tablets rattled.

"I wonder how long he has been taking these things?"

"He said about a year," said Walsh vaguely.

"Had you noticed any change in his behaviour?"

"A little. I knew he was taking something, but I had no idea what it was. He seemed a bit elevated at times. Do you really think Reid was poisoned with those things?"

"I once saw a man who had killed himself by taking too many of them," said Pat. "When he was dead he looked very like Reid. Could I have Joe in here for a few minutes? I might get something out of him if he were alone."

"Certainly." Walsh finished his drink and stood up. "I'll stay in the bar until you are finished with him."

While he waited for Joe to come, Pat looked about the office with interest. The old board floor was uncovered, and the desk and chairs were shabby. The fireplace needed new tiles here and there, and the walls and ceiling had not smelt paint for years. A huge airline calendar glared from one side of the fireplace, and on the other side a busily ticking little cuckoo clock showed the time as a quarter-past six. Pat glanced at his watch and saw that it was almost ten o'clock. At that moment a sick cuckoo came out of his little house in the clock and groaned three times. He wondered why Walsh did not keep things in better order. The whole effect was depressing, in spite of the shiny new safe and account books. It was all very much out of keeping with the rest of the hotel.

Joe's arrival did nothing to lighten the atmosphere. He had put on his apron and with his heavy gloomy face and hanging

101

hands he looked like a minor or low-grade devil employed to stoke the fires of Hell.

"Cheer up, old man," said Pat. "I won't bite you. Come over and sit down."

"No, thanks," said Joe tersely. "What do you want me for? Who's been talking about me?"

"You told me a few things in the bar, yourself," said Pat. "I just want to ask you a few questions."

"Do you care who killed Reid?" Joe asked suddenly.

"Not personally," said Pat gently, "but it's my job to care about that sort of thing. Let's begin at the beginning. Were you concerned in the agitation against Reid and his road-house?"

"I spoke at the meetings," said Joe, "if that's what you mean. And I was at the committee meeting after."

Pat raised his eyebrows. He had not known that there had been a committee at all.

"What did you say at the meeting?" he asked.

Joe told him, adding that anyone who said he had killed Reid was a liar, an informer and a Castle hack. Pat interrupted to say that no one had accused Joe of anything, and asked him for details of the committee meeting.

"We held it back of the post office," said Joe. "In Miss Byrne's place. Her sister was there, too, Mrs. Hooper, that used to be Sir Miles's housekeeper until Mr. de Cogan put her out. Damn well right, too, for she's a bitter pill, that one. Johnny Ross was there, and Barry Murphy, the blacksmith, and a few others. I might think of them all if you want to know."

"What did you talk about?"

"Well, I'll not deny we were mad anxious to have a wallop off of Reid. There was the road-house first, of course, but along with that we all had it in for him about other things. There was things he said to me in the bar the day I told him to keep away from Nora. Mr. Barne was there, and Mr. de Cogan. They'll

102

tell you. Scandalous, it was. And Mrs. Hooper seemed to think he could have stopped Mr. de Cogan from giving her the sack. She was leaving out little hints every couple of minutes and her sister was backing her up."

"What did you decide to do?"

"We made out a plan of campaign, as you might say, or the beginnings of one. Some of us had pigs and we were going to let them into his garden for a start. A pig can do terrible harm in a short while. If that didn't work we had other ideas."

"But did you want him to end by killing himself?" insisted Pat, determined to find out the philosophy behind it all.

Joe was shocked.

"Kill himself? Aren't we all Christians? And wasn't he one, too? Sure, he'd never do the like of that."

"Perhaps you drove him too far."

"We hadn't started driving him at all," Joe pointed out. "We had written him a letter, of course, but I wouldn't count that. We only said that he was to give up the plan for the road-house, and we rubbed blood off of an old rabbit on the foot of the letter, to frighten him. But that was all."

"When did you send him this letter?"

"Last night, fairly late. I brung it to the house myself and handed it over to that sour old Maggie of his."

"And you had no reply?"

"I didn't say that," said Joe sullenly.

"Then you did have a reply," said Pat patiently. "What was it? And who received it?"

"Mr. Doyle at the mill had a letter this morning——"

"You didn't tell me he was in it."

"He wasn't at the committee meeting, but he was at the other meetings, and Mr. Reid must have known that. Oh, Mr. Doyle's heart is in the right place, you can take it from me."

"No doubt," murmured Pat.

He knew Doyle for an educated, intelligent man, a university graduate too. He would never have connected him with this kind of thing. And yet Dr. Donovan had been mixed up in it, and so had Walsh, though he had not mentioned it.

"What was in the letter to Mr. Doyle?"

"He wouldn't show it to us," said Joe. "He said there was private things in it. But he said we could go ahead about the pigs. We had them all ready to let in there this evening, only we heard that Mr. Reid was dead."

This was all very plausible, but Henley could not discount the fact that Joe had certainly hated Reid. Henley thought, however, that poisoning him would have been a tame and unsatisfying business for Joe. Violence would have been more in his line, probably with plenty of blood.

Before they left the office, Pat warned Joe not to repeat their conversation to patrons of the bar. Joe looked offended, and said that he would not have dreamed of such a thing, but he looked disappointed all the same.

10

Avoiding Walsh, Henley walked meditatively upstairs and packed his belongings into his suitcase. It was too late to knock up Doyle and talk to him about his part in the agitation. A pity Reid had not died in the morning, he thought, leaving a long day for questions, and no time for people to plan their answers. Deliberately, he left his fishing-rod standing in a corner out of sight, so that he should have an excuse for coming back. Then he slipped out of the hotel and walked up the street, with the intention of re-entering Dangan House by way of the back avenue.

It was after half-past ten now. He walked on the footpath, past shut doors and bright windows. The shadow of a geranium in a pot showed on almost every drawn blind. It was all very snug and happy, and a stranger would never have guessed that in many a backyard lurked a pig who might now have been fiercely uprooting Reid's bulbs and flowers. Truly the domestic pig has many uses, Pat reflected. The mill was closed and silent when he passed by, and a single light showed in the back of Doyle's house next door.

Beyond the mill it was very dark, where the arched trees covered the starry sky. The white gate on to the avenue gleamed softly, so that he was able to open it and pass through easily. Still in deep shadow, he looked up towards the river and saw two figures standing close together on the bridge. A fine night for such diversions, he thought. The next moment he was astonished to see them break apart before first one and then the other jumped on to the river bank below. Pat shrugged. They had nothing to fear from him, even if they were trespassing. He doubted if Miles would have objected to the young men of the village taking their girls for a walk on his avenue on a summer evening. Perhaps the old man had not liked it. He walked on briskly, so that they could emerge from hiding all the sooner. Just as he had passed the bridge, however, he stopped and hesitated. He had never seen a country boy and girl behave like that before. They might blush, and turn away, and look embarrassed, but their pride would never allow them to run and hide. He put down his bag and padded back on the grassy margin of the avenue until he came to the bridge. There he stood for several minutes, almost fearing to breathe, until presently he was rewarded by a little sigh that floated up from the riverbank below him. Then a man's voice said:

"Jane! Are you all right?"

The girl's voice said breathlessly, with a little sob:

"Oh, Martin, who was it? Why should we hide, now that Tom is dead——?"

"Ssh!"

In the little scuffle that followed, Pat moved away again, as quietly as he had come. He had learned enough to be able to find out who they were, and the girl's undoubted reference to Reid's death would be ample excuse for questioning them. He promised himself that he would not unnecessarily reveal how he had learned of their connection with Reid. He grew hot all over as he recalled Joe's description of himself as a snooping policeman, remembering wryly his youthful reasons for joining the Guards. In those days he had envisaged himself in silver-buttoned magnificence standing at the corner of Grafton Street, waving on buses and trams and large shiny cars to romantic destinations. He would be the centre of all eyes, the centre of the Capital, of the whole nation. On his lordly pleasure would depend the movements of Cabinet Ministers, and even of the President himself. But, unfortunately, it had soon been discovered that he was too clever to be wasted on point-duty, and he had never even had the pleasure of waving on a wheelbarrowful of vegetables. Too late, he had learned that according to the regulations he could never be stationed within ten miles of his native town, and presently he had been transported to law-abiding Wexford where he soon took up fishing to console himself. He sighed for the grand dignified figure of his dreams.

James opened the door to his knock. "You're to go into the drawing-room," he said firmly, as Pat tried to make for the stairs. "I'll take up your bag."

And to make certain that there would be no backsliding, he opened the drawing-room door and announced that Inspector Henley was here again.

Germaine and Miles were still there, but the doctor was gone. Miles said that someone had telephoned for him and that he had left at once.

"I didn't want him any more," said Pat wearily. "I'll see him in the morning."

"Did you get your things?" Miles asked.

"Yes. James has just brought them upstairs."

"Then we can all go to bed," said Miles, looking displeased at the prospect.

"Who are Jane and Martin?" Pat asked suddenly.

"Jane Merlin," said Miles.

"Martin Doyle," said Germaine.

They looked at each other, and then inquiringly at Pat.

"Are they engaged to be married?" he asked.

"Not that I know of," said Miles. "But of course I'm not here for long. I don't know the local gossip. What do you say, Germaine?"

"You had better ask Captain Merlin," she said.

"No, no!" said Miles in distress. "That is, not unless you have to. Why not talk to the girl herself? Her father is as crazy as a coot."

"I'll talk to her in the morning," said Pat. "Have you ever seen her with Martin Doyle?"

He addressed this question to Germaine, and she answered reluctantly:

"When I lived in the lodge, I saw them once or twice pass in Martin's car, but I didn't take much notice of them."

Pat made no comment on this. It was no use harrying these people any further this evening, he thought. He took himself away to bed at last, only pausing to remind them of the presence of Carr still on guard in the library.

When Pat had gone Germaine said:

"We're very lucky to have such a friendly little man."

"Yes," said Miles absent-mindedly. "But I wonder what is all this about Jane Merlin and Martin Doyle? Why did he ask about them?"

Germaine looked uneasy.

"I don't like that," she said. "He's bound to hear about them sooner or later. Jane and Martin have been spending a lot of time together. Everyone in the village has seen that. They seem to think they have been very clever, and that it's all a deep secret. Of course we all know that the Captain wanted her to marry Reid."

"Well, she's saved from that now," said Miles, and stopped.

Suddenly a real motive for Reid's death had presented itself to him. Compared with this, the question of the road-house was a minor thing. He remembered how he himself had reacted against the idea of Jane Merlin being married to Reid. And Doyle seemed the brooding sort, who would keep a grievance and nurse it, and feed it as well as he fed his pigs in the yard behind the mill. It would have been more economical to have murdered Captain Merlin, but who could blame a man for hesitating to kill his future father-in-law? And his anger would be more naturally directed against Reid. Miles was shocked at himself for fitting Doyle so neatly into the role of murderer, without a single piece of concrete evidence. As he turned out the lights and prepared to follow Germaine upstairs, he warned himself to mind his own business.

But the day was not over yet. When he reached his room he realized that he had nothing to read. He had never in his life felt further from sleep, and on this of all nights he must have a book in which he could lose himself completely. Leaving his bedroom door open he went downstairs again. In the hall he hesitated, and then he went over and knocked firmly at the library door.

It was opened after a moment by the squirrelly Carr.

"I just want to get a book," said Miles, and walked into the room.

He stopped in astonishment. The scene before him reminded him of Hans Andersen's story, in which the farmer comes home to find his wife entertaining the local minister with a feast in the middle of the night. He managed to suppress what would have been an undignified chuckle and said mildly:

"I'm afraid I am intruding."

The library table was spread with white damask, blue and gold china, silver and glass and a quantity of food, some of which Miles recognized as the remains of dinner. But there was a glazed ham as well, and a large fruit cake and a decanter of port. And sitting in the swivel-chair by the table was Alice, the housemaid, holding a slice of ham poised on the point of a carving fork. She was so startled that she did not shriek, but her mouth was a round O of shocked surprise. The squirrel was looking sheepish now, as he held the door still and looked from Miles to Alice and back again. At last he said hurriedly:

"I'm to be here all night, Sir, and Alice was getting me a little bite of food, like."

"Good, good," said Miles, perhaps a little too heartily. Then he became embarrassed and went on quickly: "I should have thought of you myself. I'm glad Alice was able to look after you. You are already acquainted, perhaps?"

Carr blushed deeply, and nodded.

"We'll be married some time," he said, and giggled.

109

"My congratulations to you both," said Miles, reaching for Carr's reluctant hand and shaking it gravely. "You are a very lucky man. Alice will be a good provider, I can see. Tell me," he went on curiously, "don't you mind having a meal here, where Reid has so recently died?"

Carr looked surprised.

"No, Sir, I do not. Sure, a man must eat and isn't it all one to me, in a manner of speaking, where I eat?"

"And I'm thinking there won't be much feasting over Mr. Reid," said Alice mournfully, "for I hear he has hardly any relations."

"Well, don't let me disturb you," said Miles, crossing the room to the bookshelves.

They held their breath, of course, while he took a book at random and watched him to the door, where he turned to wish them good night.

"Good night, Sir, good night, good night," said Carr, nearly biting off his tongue in his excitement.

"Good night, Sir," said Alice slowly and sweetly.

On his way upstairs, he wondered if he should have shown some displeasure at the lavish display of Alice's affection for Carr, at his expense. But he could only feel gratitude to them for lightening his humour. Perhaps in time he might even be able to put the whole incident of Reid's death out of his mind altogether. It could be done by severe mental discipline, or by copying the delightfully airy attitude of Alice. He would discuss it all with Germaine in the morning.

In bed at last, he opened his book and found, to his amusement, that it was *The Wind in the Willows*. Presently he found himself sympathizing with the Badger, who simply hated Society, who "trotted forward a pace or two, then grunted, 'H'm! Company,' and turned his back and disappeared from view".

"That's exactly what I feel like doing," said Miles to himself.

The book was soothing, and he fell asleep at last, to dream of squirrels in blue uniforms and badgers in grey tweed suits and himself frantically trying to get them all lined up and counted for some obscure but intensely exciting reason. When he awoke in the morning he was physically and mentally exhausted.

11

The sight of Barne at the breakfast table did nothing to stimulate him. He sat there, small and drooping like a jackdaw, but Miles noticed that he was eating quite a large breakfast. Germaine appeared a moment later, with Henley to open the door for her. Miles found himself a little more cheerful as they all sat down together.

"I suppose I had better visit Reid's house this morning," said Pat presently. "It's the gate just beyond the village, I think?"

"Yes. He christened it Fairy Lawn," said Germaine. "Not many fairies about, though. If there had been, Reid would have clipped them in two. He was a demon with the clippers, all straight lines and flat surfaces."

Barne looked offended.

"I think he had made the place very nice, very nice indeed," he said stiffly.

"Of course," said Germaine quickly. "He had done wonderful work there." She turned eagerly to Pat. "Do you remember it before Reid came? It looked like a man who hadn't shaved for a long time. Well, Reid shaved it, that's all."

She looked meditatively at her plate and Miles noticed that she flushed a little. He hated Barne for embarrassing her. Obviously, she felt that her last remark had not improved matters. He wondered how soon they would be rid of that wretched but useful little man. He could never understand how Barne could have described Germaine as a typical old maid. On the contrary, Miles thought that she had an unusual mind which worked in a series of delightfully stimulating images. Certainly, something about her irritated Barne, so that in her company he became dull and prosy. The spark that Miles had noticed in him on the first day they had met was quite extinguished.

French windows from the dining-room opened out on to a sunny gravelled path, and as soon as they had finished breakfast Pat and Miles walked out into the garden. Barne was still eagerly nibbling toast, and lifting the lid of the coffee-pot to see if any drop remained. Germaine had cut her breakfast short and had gone to see about the housekeeping, so she said.

"I wonder who is at Reid's house?" Miles said.

"I have had a man there since last night," said Pat. "And there is the housekeeper who did the cooking, too, and a man-servant, called Georgie Fahy."

Miles felt deflated by this spate of information. The Guards were so depressingly businesslike. Pat seemed to sense the effect of his words for he said apologetically:

"We have our own methods of handling this sort of thing. Try not to think about it too much. Just leave the grisly details to me."

So he thinks I'm a big softie, thought Miles in annoyance. It was so near the truth that he was stung to use an airy, careless tone as he said:

"Did you know that Captain Merlin had plans for his daughter to marry Reid?"

Pat stopped, surprised.

"Plans? Surely girls marry who they please these days."

"I don't think that is as true as is generally supposed," said Miles. "A young girl's conscience might force her into obeying even as cracked a father as Merlin. If a very strong reason were adduced, she might take on his sins, as it were——"

"What do you mean by that? Have you some knowledge of this reason?"

"No, no. I hardly know what I mean myself. I'm just thinking aloud. There is something ugly there, I'm convinced of that. It may have something to do with Reid's death."

Pat walked down to the village after Miles had left him rather abruptly. He knew Merlin by sight, and had once had a drink with him in the hotel bar. The sight of the Captain's nauseating mixture of stout and rum had rather put him off seeking his company on other occasions. It was half-past nine now, almost too early to visit anyone, but when he reached Merlin's house he opened the gate and walked up the little flagged path to the door. As he stood in the tiled porch he turned to observe the perfection of the little garden. Not a weed showed anywhere, not so much as a daisy in the closely mown grass. There was a low rock-garden at one side with miniature shrubs and glittering little flowering plants. An herbaceous border stretched from the gate to the house, its edges cut clean and sharp and the earth between the tall plants raked smooth.

"Good morning, Mr. Henley," said Jane Merlin's voice behind him.

She had opened the door so silently that he had not heard her, and now she stood there looking at him nervously, jerking her head and trying to smile. He apologized for calling so early and said a few conventional words in praise of her garden. She responded without enthusiasm. He was not surprised that she knew who he was, of course, but there was something a little challenging in the way in which she had not even pretended to need an introduction. There was no mistaking the fear that stared like a little devil from behind her eyes, but he was convinced that the nervous jerk of the head had not been acquired since yesterday. He supposed that she would be called a pretty girl, with that little square head and fair hair, but Pat rarely saw beauty that did not come from a soul at peace, and to him she was almost revoltingly ugly.

"I thought that as you were Mr. Reid's neighbour you might be able to tell me something about him—whether he was in good spirits lately, and so on."

"Perhaps you would like to speak to my father," she said.

Without waiting for an answer she darted across the hall and opened the door of a room that looked out on the front garden.

"Inspector Henley is here," she said abruptly.

She ran upstairs, leaving him to go into the room and shut the door behind him as best he might.

This was obviously the Captain's room, if one were to judge from the grey dullness of the furnishings, the carpet and the curtains, which almost matched his terrible tweed suit. He was sitting at a table near the window with a pile of unopened newspapers in front of him. When he stood up to shake hands, Pat found that he had to look up into his face. He had not realized that Merlin was such a tall man, though he could see that this was one reason why he looked so very odd. His extreme thinness made him look even taller, and his wild fair hair added a touch of the ridiculous. But there was nothing ridiculous about his cruel blue eyes, nor about his hard mouth, both of which now showed cold anger. He was trying to cover his feelings, but they came out in every move that he made.

"Sit down," he said curtly. Then with an effort: "Nice day."

Pat agreed that it was, and then was silent. He always let this kind of person take the lead in talk. Merlin's hands twitched.

"First bit of damn sunshine this year," he went on. "I'm stiff. Arthritis. Look at my hands." Pat did so and shuddered. "Got gold injections for it. Had to inject plenty of gold into the doctor too, ha-ha."

"Ha-ha," said Pat politely.

"Terrible climate in Ireland. England is just as bad. Wish to God I could get away to somewhere warm."

"That's what we'd all like," said Pat and waited again.

"Terrible thing about Reid," said Merlin impatiently. "That's what you've come about, I suppose. My daughter was engaged to him. Very bad for her, all this. Innocent simple young girl, you know."

In my eye, thought Pat. Her heart is not broken in quite that way.

"They were going to be married very soon," said Merlin. "Don't know what I'll do about her now."

"You needn't worry about her," said Pat airily. "A good-looking girl like that is sure to attract a husband."

"Not necessarily a husband to my liking," said Merlin peevishly. He made a great effort to make his tone that of a solicitous father as he went on: "Mother's dead, you see. No one to look after the girl but me. I won't last long in this climate. I'd be all right in the Canary Islands or in Spain perhaps. Tom Reid was a good fellow. He would have looked after—her. Don't know what I'll do now."

"Is there anything in the papers about Reid's death?" asked Pat, glancing casually at the pile on the table.

"Haven't opened them yet," said Merlin. He glanced furtively at the papers and did not offer them to Pat. "About Reid," he said, hitching himself forward in his chair. "You know he was murdered?"

"I haven't quite made up my mind yet," said Pat. "It could have been suicide."

Merlin gave a short, sour laugh.

"Suicide? Why? What had he to complain of? He had money, and a fine house, and he was going to be married. Now if it were me it would be different." He stopped to contemplate and then he shivered. "Yes, if it were me one could understand it. But not Reid."

"Who would murder him, I wonder?"

"I can think of someone who would," said Merlin. "Doyle. Do you know him? Manages Dangan Mills. Nice little salary depending on de Cogan's good will. Could be out of his job to-morrow. Talks about pig-food all the time."

"Why should he murder Reid?"

"To get my daughter Jane for himself, of course," said Merlin. "Fellow had the nerve to come here and ask me for her. I answered him, all right."

He laughed sourly again. Pat said gently:

116

"Did Reid ask you for her too?"

"Yes," said Merlin eagerly. "Though Reid was a self-made man, he had a gentlemanly way about him. Always knew the right thing to do. Before he said a word to Jane he came and asked me if I had any objection to him as a son-in-law."

Shrewd Reid, thought Henley, who was beginning to see how Merlin's mind worked.

"And what did you say?" he asked gently.

Merlin smirked to himself.

"Oh, I had a talk to him about finances. Have to think of these things, you know. He was very well off. He showed me his bank-book. Had it ready in his pocket, as a matter of fact." Pat could see that Merlin's mouth watered at the thought of it.

"I got five hundred pounds off him there and then," said Merlin softly and reverently.

Pat had just been congratulating himself on his insight into Merlin's mind, but this last statement took him completely by surprise. He experienced a feeling of physical shock, as if he had fallen heavily. He had seen Merlin's greed and the fact that his interest in Reid's money had not been entirely on his daughter's account. He had even seen that Merlin would have made a specific arrangement for himself at Reid's expense, after the marriage, but he had never imagined that he would make a demand before Reid and his daughter had become engaged. Fortunately, Merlin was not looking at him. He was looking greedily into the empty fireplace, rubbing his hands and gloating like a professional miser.

"We knew where we were then, you see," he went on. "I told him I would encourage Jane to take an interest in him, and that I would spend some of the money on clothes for her. He would have given me more later. He said he would." Suddenly he stopped and looked at Pat sideways. "Are you shocked at this? It's an old-fashioned away of doing things, but a good way. I wouldn't tell you at all only that I want to show you that Reid wouldn't have killed himself. He had made a down payment.

117

He was a business man. He hadn't yet collected the goods."

"That is so," said Pat.

He was thinking that though Merlin was angry he should have been angrier than he was at Reid's murder, because now there would be no more payments to him. He seemed more like a man who had suffered a set-back, but who is determined not to be vanquished. That was it. He was angry, but he was not in despair. The conclusions to be drawn from this were shocking.

Pat could understand now why Jane Merlin was so distracted. He could imagine the scene between her and her father, in which it was explained to her that she was to be sold to Reid. He could imagine her contempt, her refusal, and finally her breakdown and surrender when Merlin told her that he had already taken money from Reid. Miles de Cogan had guessed at some of this, Pat thought, when he had said that a conscientious young girl might take on the sin of her father. The little conversation that Pat had overheard on the bridge last night now began to fit into the pattern.

But Jane had not the look of a self-sacrificing daughter. This could be because she had no intention of being sacrificed although she had given a verbal consent. She might, for instance, have decided to save herself by the bold stroke of poisoning Reid. For all her little, light frame, she was no weak woman. It does not take much physical strength to slip a few tablets into a man's drink. And Reid would have trusted her. Pat had no doubt that she had not wanted for opportunities. She lived next door to Reid, and it seemed likely that she visited him there often.

Merlin was saying peevishly:

"You take my advice, young man, and get after Doyle. Little upstart."

"What does Miss Merlin think?" asked Pat gently.

"She's heartbroken. Dammit, man, her fiancé is dead. She doesn't think. She's shattered."

But his hands twitched again.

118

"You're planning something," thought Pat as he got up to go. "I don't know what it is, but you're planning something."

He shook hands with Merlin and went towards the door.

"Come and tell me how you are getting on," said the Captain. "I'll be interested to know."

He did not come out into the hall. Pat let himself out and slipped around to the window for a moment to look in at the unconscious Merlin. He was scrabbling through his newspapers with an hysterical energy. Pat walked down the path and let himself out through the gate. There was something odd, almost indecent, in the perfection of that garden, he thought, as if the girl who tended it had been desperately seeking an outlet for her feelings. She had not seemed interested in it for its own sake. Otherwise she would surely have led him about and told him the Christian name of every plant, as gardening enthusiasts had often done to him before. He thought it possible that her father was behind the gardening, too, in spite of the dismal room in which Pat had found him. It would be like him to think that gardening was a suitable occupation for a young girl, and an advertisement for her capabilities as a housewife. Pat felt deeply sorry for Jane. He himself was sensitive enough to be disturbed even by the few minutes he had spent with the crazy Captain. Her life with him must surely be an unending torment. Nevertheless, if she had poisoned Reid, his business was to indict her, and let a soft-hearted judge and jury do what they liked afterwards.

12

As he walked up the avenue to Reid's house, he noticed the same perfection in the grounds in a bigger and therefore less obvious way. "Suburban" was the word that occurred to him. The very tufts of daffodil leaves still standing flowerless looked as if their hair had been parted in the middle. The house was a little gem, but far too clean and neat for Pat's taste. Never a swallow would dare to nest in those eaves, nor a swarm of wild bees to set up house in the spare bedroom. The huge torso of Lawlor hovering at the drawing-room window struck an incongruous note. He came out and opened the front door. As they went into the drawing-room, Pat said:

"I'm later than I meant to be. I've been calling on Merlin. Do you know him?"

"I do. He's one of my parishioners. Cracked, of course. There's something about a picturesque Irish village that attracts his kind. We never know what to make of them. Sometimes I think they're not real people at all. I'm always afraid I'll get like them myself."

"That's one thing you need never fear," said Pat, keeping a straight face, in sympathy with Lawlor's troubled expression. "What news have you? Have you found anything interesting?"

"I have," said Lawlor. "One or two things. And there's a report on Reid's insides."

"That's very quick. What do they say?"

"Nicotine."

"As in cigarettes?"

"Yes, but they suggested that an insecticide was used. There

120

is a mixture for killing the greenfly on roses that contains any amount of it."

"But wouldn't Reid have tasted it?"

"It would have a strong, pungent taste, but if he took it in whisky he mightn't have noticed it. And he always tossed back his whisky in one gulp, which would make it very much easier."

"So it wasn't Joe's benzedrine after all," said Henley.

He felt a little guilty now at having frightened Joe, but on the other hand he could not have helped feeling pleased at the things he had learned as a result.

"We won't be in a hurry to tell everyone how Reid died," he said, and he told Lawlor about last night's conversation with Joe.

"Reid didn't grow many roses," Lawlor went on, "so he would hardly have nicotine about the place. I've been poking about to see would I find some all the same. There's an old tiger of a housekeeper below in the kitchen, but I looked around in spite of her."

"It seems unlikely that he drank nicotine by accident if it was not kept in the house," said Henley. "The trouble is that nearly everyone in Dangan has a garden of some sort, so that any of them might have the stuff. He had a very nice place here," he went on, looking around the room.

Like Miles, he was pained by the pictures, but he had learned more tolerance than Miles. Lawlor went across and opened a small drawer in the little writing desk.

"Look what I found," he said, holding out a glittering object on his huge palm.

Pat took it, and brought it over to the window to examine it. It was a platinum ring with a huge solitaire diamond, a vulgar, showy thing, and certainly the sort of ring that Reid would favour. Engraved on the inside was the name *Jane*.

"Well, well," said Henley softly. "Where does this lead us?"

"Jane is Miss Merlin, of course," said Lawlor. "I'd like to know what it proves. It could be either of two things."

121

"That she returned the ring yesterday and that he poisoned himself in despair——"

"Or that he had not yet given it to her, and therefore would not have poisoned himself at all."

"Was there a box?" asked Pat.

There was a tiny ivory one with the name of an expensive Dublin jeweller inside the lid. The ring looked completely new, as if it had never been worn at all. In any case, it was such a flashy thing that the girl could not have worn it unnoticed. But she could have had it in her possession without wearing it in public. Her father had said positively that she had been engaged to Reid, and that surely implied a ring.

Lawlor said:

"The other thing I found is a draft of a will."

"A will! I certainly did not expect that. What does it say? Who made it for him? Where is it?"

"Easy on, sir," said Lawlor, who was beginning to look flustered. "I'm one of those chaps that can only think of one thing at a time."

"Sorry. I didn't mean to fuss you. Just tell me about it yourself."

"I found it thrown on the desk among a few other papers. It's dated about six weeks ago. He wrote it himself—just said this was his last will and he revokes all other wills and codicils, and he leaves his holdings in stocks whatsoever and his money in the bank and his house property except this house to Miss Jane Merlin who is soon to be his wife."

"And the house?"

"To Mr. Barne, that little pysawn of a solicitor that was so friendly with him. You remember him—he was up at Dangan House last night. Fidgeting around like a clocking hen."

"I remember him," said Pat. "Is that all it says?"

"There's something about Mr. Barne appreciating the house so much, and a few bequests to the servants. That's all, really. The only snag is that it's not signed."

"Wasn't it a queer thing to leave the house to a man much older than himself?" Pat commented. "In fact, it's a very queer document in every way. I'll have to go back and have another chat with old Merlin."

"He didn't mention the brother in Limerick at all," said Lawlor. "A decent man—a cousin of mine has a shop in the same place. Reid wasn't on speaking terms with his brother, so it's no wonder he left him nothing."

"If Reid made no other will, the brother will probably get everything," said Henley.

He had found the draft will on the desk and was reading through it eagerly.

"He's very glib about revoking all other wills and codicils," he went on, "but that's no proof there is another in existence. We'll have to keep our eyes open for one."

Lawlor led him all over the house and grounds. They questioned the servants as they met them, with an apparent casualness that would not have deceived a child. Miss Maggie Murphy was the tigress in the kitchen, and she made it clear that her opinion of the Guards could not have been lower.

"Of course some people say they're all right," she said disdainfully, looking over their heads. "But I say they'll never be like the old R.I.C. Never. My brother was in the old R.I.C. and he always said the same up to the day he died. And as for the London policemen, he always used to say they were wonderful. Those were his very words."

"Now where have I heard that before?" said Pat thoughtfully.

Henley prodded her on to further remarks of the same sort, but he had to give it up presently because there was nothing there relevant to the case in hand. Miss Murphy had beautiful soft white hair and a pair of narrow, meanly slanting eyes. She had not expressed the smallest interest in Reid's fate. She had been out all the afternoon yesterday, having taken the bus to Dublin to do some shopping, so she knew nothing of Reid's movements, she said. When they had left her Lawlor said:

"It's easy to see how she's a Miss at this hour of her life. Sour old jade."

They found Georgie Fahy cutting the grass of a smooth lawn at the side of the house. He was small, with sooty black hair and a pointed face. His eyes were smoke-grey, dancing with intelligence which he took no trouble to conceal. His age could have been anything from thirty to forty-five. He seemed rather pleased with Reid's end.

"Not that I wished him ill, God rest him," he said piously, "but he was a terrible man to work for. Like a flea, always hopping from one thing to another. There was no pleasing him."

Georgie said that he had been gardener and handyman and houseman and chauffeur.

"A quick-change artist I was, sir," he said. "I had a uniform for every one of those jobs, and I had to be in and out of them all day long. Often I saw visitors staring at me when they'd see me pouring out tea in a white jacket five minutes after I had been driving the car in breeches and gaiters. I nearly had ulsters from it all and that's no lie. I wouldn't wish Mr. Reid ill, do you understand me now, but at the same time I'm glad there is an end to my job here."

Remembering James MacDonagh who worked for Miles, Henley asked:

"Did you have anything to do with the agitation against Mr. Reid's road-house?"

"No, sir," said Georgie firmly. "I was asked, of course, but I wouldn't have cut, shuffle nor deal to do with it. I'm not a Dangan man at all, you see, and I don't take all that interest in what goes on here."

"Where are you from?" asked Pat.

"County Kerry," said Georgie, and he named the village. "It's down by the sea, and there's ne'er a captain nor a colonel could live in it, for they'd be blown out of it with the first storm. I used to work in the hotel down there, but then I used to be out of a job in the winter time, so I got into this racket instead."

He jerked his head in the direction of the house.

"How did Mr. Reid take all this agitation against him, the meetings and so on? Did it worry him? Or do you think he thought of giving in?"

"At first I thought he'd give in," said Georgie judicially. "He looked a bit shook, and he didn't go out much for a couple of days, only rambling around the place here looking like the wrath of God. Then all of a sudden he got fighting mad, till I thought he'd get a stroke. I seen him there the night before last taking out the young horse he bought last winter and galloping him off like the Charge of the Light Brigade. I thought the horse would be in bits when I'd see him again, but by the mercy of God he survived it."

"Which way did he go? Did he ride through the village?"

"No, he did not, then. Sure, he knew there was a meeting going on down there. 'Twas in the other direction he went. I was trotting a duck out that way a while after and I saw him come out of the gate of Dangan House—Mr. de Cogan's place, you know."

"I know," said Pat softly. This was interesting news. "What did you say you were doing out there yourself?"

Georgie got very red in the face.

"There's no law against it that I ever heard," he said truculently. "Why wouldn't I take my girl out for a respectable walk of a fine summer evening——"

"I beg your pardon," Pat interrupted hastily. "I just didn't understand you for a moment. Would the young lady mind telling me her own impression of the meeting?"

"She'll do what I say," said Georgie firmly. "We have an understanding, you see, though her Pa doesn't know about it yet. I'll tell her she can answer all your questions. Mind you, we didn't exactly *meet* Mr. Reid. We kept out of sight. 'Twas

125

safer not to be in his way, with the way he was handling the horse."

"What is your young lady's name?" asked Pat, who had his notebook and pencil out.

"Miss Nora Connolly. She lives in the village. Her father is Joe Connolly in the hotel bar. She's young yet, but by next year she'll be ready for the market."

Pat put his notebook back in his pocket and drew a deep breath before he said carefully:

"You say her father doesn't know you have been going out together?"

"That's right, sir. You know Joe, and the way he carries on about Nora. You'd think she's still in the cradle. There's plenty of go in Nora, though, and I'm saying it. He should be glad to get her into safe hands, for she'd be a flyer if she got off on her own."

Pat made no comment on this, since Georgie seemed so pleased. He said:

"Will Joe call you safe hands for his Nora now, if you have no job?"

"Oh, that will be all right," said Georgie airily. "I'll fix all that with him when the time comes. Myself and Nora has it all planned. We got the idea from Mr. Reid. We'll open a road-house of our own, and put Joe working in the bar—why do you look so surprised, sir?"

"It's all a bit confusing," said Pat apologetically. "I thought Joe disapproves of road-houses."

"It will be different when he has one of his own," said Georgie with the philosophy of all the ages.

Lawlor had kept silent throughout this conversation. As they moved away from Georgie, who had his mower going again, he said, putting his finger on the most interesting point that had emerged:

"I wonder if Reid visited Mr. de Cogan on the night before he died?"

"Mr. de Cogan didn't mention his visit to me," said Pat, "I'm going back to visit Captain Merlin again, to ask him about that ring. Meanwhile, you could look about for nicotine."

"I'll do that," said Lawlor with a sigh. "Will you mention the will to Merlin?"

"I think it would be worth while," said Henley. "He's going to be very sore about it, especially if he has had the trouble of poisoning Reid for nothing."

13

Leaving Lawlor standing open-mouthed on Reid's front steps, Pat started down the avenue. He was thinking how fortunate it was that he had spent so many careless holidays in Dangan. Without knowing it, he had assimilated a considerable amount of knowledge and understanding of the village and its inhabitants, without which he would have been greatly hampered. There was a sort of coy, closed-in self-sufficiency about Dangan which he would have found quite intimidating if this had been his first visit. He remembered how he had crept down the street on that first day clutching his fishing-rod, trying to make himself invisible until he had reached open country. Thinking about it later, he could hardly remember what it was that had made him so uneasy, unless it was the always unnerving mixture of sporting gentry and watchful natives. Standing long hours in the river, waiting for a bite, he had gradually become less sensitive, though he had always been acutely aware of the old-fashioned feudal atmosphere.

He admired Lawlor for his impartial attitude. To him a farm labourer with an unlit bicycle and a drunken gentleman driving home from a hunt ball were simply two bipeds breaking the law. He would prosecute both with equal implacability. But though this approach was practical for everyday purposes, Pat doubted if it would do in this case. One might put it that most of the offences with which Lawlor would have to deal were objective. Murder was surely a subjective one. Only one person in thousands saw murder as a solution to his difficulties, or reckoned that the satisfaction of killing his enemy would be worth the consequent uneasiness and fear of apprehension.

Unless by a highly improbable coincidence, only one person in this neighbourhood would be psychologically capable of killing Reid. It was in judging this angle of the affair that Pat hoped to find his knowledge of the Dangan people useful.

For the second time that morning he walked up the path to Merlin's house. It was like a snail's house, he thought, so neat and shining on the outside but inhabited by a peering, slimy creature. The front door stood open, and no one came in answer to his ring. He knew that Merlin employed no staff of any kind, and that Jane did all the housework herself. Pat reflected that she was not very good at it, as he noticed the dusty hall and stairs.

Just then she came around by the side of the house, with a trowel in her hand. She was wearing big gardening gloves, which somehow seemed to confirm his conclusion that she did not like gardening. He had a fixed conviction that real addicts have a positive liking for grubbing in the earth and feeling the damp worms slip by under their bare fingers. His own tastes did not include gardening.

She looked startled for a moment when she saw him standing there, and then she came towards him slowly, with the trowel hanging from her hand. She answered his ingratiating smile with a frightened stare as she stammered:

"You want to see my father again. He went out, just after you left."

"Where did he go?" Pat asked gently.

"I don't know. He didn't say." By a tremendous effort she got her voice under control and her lip curled—in anger at herself, Pat thought. "Could you come back later? Or can I do anything for you?"

"Yes. Could we go inside?"

Leaving the gloves and the trowel in the porch, she led him through the hall to a dining-room at the back of the house. A basket of mending, a pile of magazines, one or two blown-glass ornaments over the fireplace, led him to the conclusion that she used this room as a sitting-room for herself. The curtains were clean and pretty and the furniture dusted and polished as if she took more care with it than with the rest of the house. The small dining table by the window held a bowl of roses.

"I'm afraid you were ringing for some time," she said jerkily, as soon as they were seated. "I left the housework this morning to do some gardening. It's such a fine morning."

"Do you like gardening?" he asked conversationally.

"It's all right in fine weather," she said in a bitter tone, "but I detest it in early spring and in the autumn. I get so cold and miserable."

"Why do you grow so many flowers then? Why not just have a border of flowers and the rest in grass?"

"My father likes it this way," she said, trying to sound as if that was enough reason for her to devote her time to it.

But she hates it, and she hates her father, thought Pat, and the latter revelation appalled him.

"I'm sorry to have to question you so soon after your fiancé's death," he said, watching her carefully. "I have just been in his house, and we found one or two things."

"What did you find? Tell me! What did you find?"

"We found a valuable diamond ring with the name *Jane* engraved on the inside of it," said Pat smoothly.

She stared wildly for a moment and then burst into a little high laugh. Then she covered her mouth with her hand like a child, and looked at him over her fingers. He said:

"Was it your engagement ring?"

"I had no ring," she said in a hysterical tone.

Suddenly Pat became alarmed lest she might have a real fit of hysterics the very next moment, alone in the house with him. He dropped his pose of gentle, wondering innocence and said sharply:

"Pull yourself together please! Put your hands down."

She did so, and sat staring at him. He went on:

"Now, this is not the moment for playing tricks. If you don't answer my questions now you'll have to do so later. You may as well get it over."

She nodded slowly, clutching her hands together in her lap. She was very far gone, he thought in despair, and wondered whether she were capable of telling the truth even if she wanted to.

"You were engaged to be married to Thomas Reid," he began. "Your father told me so."

She nodded and said in a low voice:

"Yes, I had become engaged to him."

"When?"

"Last week. It had been talked about for some time, but it was only settled last week."

He noticed that she spoke about it impersonally, as if it had had nothing to do with her.

"But you had no ring?"

"I didn't want one. I said I wouldn't have one until—until later on. But my father wanted it. He has old-fashioned ideas."

Very politely put, thought Pat. Her father had wanted everything tied up neatly.

"So Mr. Reid got a ring to please your father?"

"Oh, no," she said, seeing no irony in the question. "Mr. Reid had always wanted me to have a ring, but he only bought it when my father asked him to."

She turned her eyes down, and he saw her flush with embarrassment. He warned himself not to give way to sympathy for her lest he lose his present clear-sighted point of view.

"So you knew he had bought the ring?"

She stopped for a moment, and Pat saw with annoyance that she was running back over the conversation in her mind, trying to remember how much she had said. He asked suddenly:

"When did Reid give you the ring?"

"He never gave it to me at all," she said in a half-whisper.

"Surely he gave it to you last week, and you returned it to him yesterday when you broke off your engagement to him."

"No, no, no! He never gave it to me. I never broke off my engagement to him. My father——"

She stopped. Pat said meditatively:

"Your father would never have allowed you to break off your engagement."

She looked at him helplessly, and angry tears came into her eyes. After a moment she nodded.

"You seem to know more than I thought," she said drearily.

"I'm sorry," said Pat quickly. "But I must find out the truth. Would you like to change anything you have said?"

"No, I have said nothing but the truth. Mr. Reid had not given me that ring, though I knew that he had bought it."

"Did you know that your name was engraved on the inside of the ring?"

Pat noticed that she never used Reid's Christian name. She spoke of him as if he had been her employer, he thought. Now she said:

"Of course I didn't know that my name was on the ring, I had never seen the ring at all. Mr. Reid told me one day that he was going to buy it. He—he measured my finger for it."

She looked at her left hand and shuddered. Henley said, deliberately callous:

"Well, you don't have to worry about that any more, since he's dead. Why did he not give you the ring?"

"I don't know."

"Did you expect him to? Did you ask him about it?"

"*Ask* him! Oh, God!"

"Very well, then. You didn't ask him. But you must have wondered why he didn't come and give it to you on the evening of the day he bought it."

Now she was twitching her hands again, and turning her head from side to side as if she were thinking of darting past him out of the room. Suddenly Pat was struck by an inspiration.

"Did you think your father had something to do with it?"

She nodded miserably, but said nothing.

"Did you think that your father was holding Reid up for more money before he would allow Reid to give you the ring?"

Suddenly she was on her feet, shrieking at him.

"Yes, yes! That's what I thought. Very nice, isn't it? Very interesting for you to find out! Won't it make a funny story to tell your friends, you interfering, curious little upstart!"

"Sit down, please," said Henley sharply. "We'll finish the whole business in another few minutes."

She sat down shakily, looking at him with rage and hatred.

"I don't discuss the details of my work for the amusement of my friends," he said carefully. "And anyway yours is not a very amusing story. You have been despicably treated and I have no intention of making life more difficult for you than it already is." She drew a long breath, and seemed to relax a little. Pat went on: "I think you were wrong in your guess at the reason why you were not given the ring. Your father told me himself that he had asked Reid for five hundred pounds at the beginning of Reid's attentions to you. He thought he had been very clever. Don't you think he would have told me if he had asked for more at the time of your formal engagement?"

"He might not have told you," she said huskily. "Perhaps Mr. Reid refused to give it to him."

So that's what she thinks, thought Pat, that Reid refused to pay more and that her father then poisoned him. If this was so, no wonder she was in a state of terror. He paused to work out how to put his next question:

"How did Reid behave towards you between the date of his buying the ring and the day that he died?"

"He was quite different from what he had been before," she said. "I could not make out what had happened. I thought—what I said. I almost thought he was giving up—becoming less interested in me."

"Did you see much of him?"

"I saw him every evening. That was the arrangement. He was

133

very polite, but I thought he had become—more distant. I was glad of that," she finished wearily.

They sat in silence for a few moments while he thought out the implications of what she had told him. Something had happened in the last week to shake Reid in his determination to marry Jane Merlin. It could have been that he had realized how unwilling she was, but Pat thought it unlikely that this would have been sufficient reason for Reid. With his arrogant self-confidence, he would have been certain that he would have been able to charm her eventually. Besides, she had continued up to the last to fall in with her father's wishes, and had agreed to accept Reid's ring. Whether she would have actually gone through with the marriage was a speculation that Pat was glad to be able to ignore.

He looked at her now, sitting there all crumpled, like a thrush after the cats have had it, and wondered if it would be safe to ask her the rest of his questions. At last he decided that it would be harder for her if he had to come back and question her again.

"Did you know about Reid's will?" he asked softly.

She did. He knew it the moment she turned wild blue eyes on him again. And it was because of the will that she suspected her father of having murdered Reid. He could see her trying to make up her mind whether to admit that she had known about it or not. He did not care how she answered, he was so certain that she had known.

"Mr. Reid's will?" she said.

"Yes," said Henley conversationally. "We found a will there, leaving all his money and property, except the house, to you."

"Oh!" She was too exhausted to succeed in looking surprised. "My father will be pleased."

How very thoroughly she was under her father's influence, thought Henley. He even wondered if it were possible that her father had instructed her to poison Reid. Her father was capable of it, but she would have resisted him to the limit there, he was certain. And Captain Merlin was a clever man, for all his oddities and incredible meanness, and he would have been likely to assess his daughter's strength before trying to push her so far. At this point Pat pulled himself up sharply. He had been seriously following up a line so fantastic as to be almost outside the bounds of possibility. These crazy people would have him reduced to their own state soon, if he were not careful.

"Did your father know about the will?" he asked.

"Knowing my father, how can you ask that?" she said bitterly.

"Did he make Reid draw up that will? Look at me, please, Miss Merlin. Did your father ask Reid to make that will?"

She made a hopeless gesture with her hand.

"What's the use? You know so much. Yes, he asked Mr. Reid to make the will, in case he might die before we were married. My father is not very subtle about these things. Mr. Reid was laughing about it. I heard him. He brought the will here one day and showed it to my father. I didn't see it at all. I didn't want to. My father was delighted that day, though he told me that Mr. Reid had not done it exactly as he had wanted it."

He would not have liked the part about leaving the house to Barne, Henley thought. He imagined Reid putting in that piece to annoy the Captain, and to show him that he could not go too far with his outrageous demands. Reid was no weakling, and Henley was reasonably sure that he had never intended to sign the will. He watched Jane's face intently as he remarked casually:

"Of course the will is worth nothing. Reid had not signed it."

Her reaction was astonishing. She leaped up, her eyes shining, triumph and delight in her face. She looked as most people would if they heard that they had won first prize in the Irish Sweep. Pat smiled in spite of himself at her pleasure.

"Thank God! Oh, thank God!" she chattered. "Isn't it wonderful——"

She stopped and tried to control herself, but she could not suppress a wide, almost childlike grin. Perhaps there was some hope for her, he thought. Martin Doyle was welcome to what was left of a potentially beautiful and happy girl, who had been warped and twisted until only occasional glimpses of the original material remained.

He left her then, swearing her to secrecy about the whole conversation, and warning her especially not to mention the will to her father at all. The look of triumph became ugly as she said sourly:

"I won't tell him. I don't sit and chat with him anyway."

Convention made her come to the door with him and say a few polite things as he turned away. He glanced back before he reached the gate, and was just in time to see her give the little pile of gardening gloves and trowel an ill-tempered and quite unmaidenly kick.

"Yes, Martin Doyle can have her," he said to himself.

But he was honest enough with himself to admit that he could understand what they saw in her.

14

Miles had a deadly sense of anticlimax that morning. Germaine had become preoccupied with household business, and he caught one glimpse of her standing among piles of linen with Alice, in the linen-room. He saw the local Guards padding purposefully about. They looked uncomfortable every time they caught his eye, so that he did his best to avoid them. Inspector Henley was having an interesting time at Reid's house, no doubt. At least he had left Dangan House early and had not come back. Even Barne would have served for company, but he had muttered something about putting in the time usefully, and had gone into the little estate office off the hall and had shut the door.

Miles rambled around to the farmyard. It was such a delightfully sunny morning that it was hard to realize the grim truth of yesterday's events. He was glad to find that he had not yet lived long enough in Dangan to be much concerned personally about Reid's death. He had tried very hard to become a part of the village, but fortunately for himself he had not quite succeeded. The rank odour of violence hung about the place, for all that, and penetrated his detachment.

He found John Wall in one of the cool, wide coach-houses, instructing one of the men in the cleansing of a tractor. Miles found himself taking a certain pleasure in his power to call John away, so that they could talk over the new plans for the mill. Between them, John and Doyle had spoken to every one of the mill-workers, and had met with an astonishing amount of enthusiasm. Most of the men were only one generation removed from the land, and they had the Irish countryman's power to grasp and appreciate an abstract idea. Many of them were interested in the co-operative movement already, but had never dreamed that it could be put to work in Dangan. The good land was still firmly in the hands of the gentlemen, and while the prices of farm produce remained as high as they were, there was no likelihood that the farms would not be worked. Generally speaking, there was little prospect of the Land Commission taking over the estates and dividing the land out among the people, as long as a reasonable proportion of it was tilled. The Dangan people did not particularly covet the land, in any case. They were often exasperated at the highhanded attitude of the estate owners, but they usually dismissed the whole seed and breed of them with a tolerant shrug, and the comforting prophecy that they were dying out.

The mill was another story, however. They felt that it belonged to them, and they had often seen how their personal fortunes depended on it. To be allowed to have a hand, however small, in the direction of those fortunes was enough to make every man hold his head higher. Soon, John said, they would be calling it "Our Mill", and soon after that, he added sardonically, they would begin to fall out about shares, and ownership, and hereditary rights of all kinds.

"So the sooner we have a legal document to show them, the better," he said. "Once they see it down in black and white, they won't argue any more, and then the business of developing the mill can go ahead."

"I haven't had a chance of talking to Mr. Barne since he arrived," said Miles. "I wrote to him after our first conversation, and asked him to get out some kind of a draft agreement that we could start with. But immediately after he reached here, poor Mr. Reid was found dead, and I have had no opportunity for talking to him since then. He may have brought down the draft with him. I don't want to harry him just now, because he's all upset about Reid. A day or two won't matter to us."

138

Wall agreed that there was no need to be in too much of a hurry.

"Mr. Doyle is like a cat with two tails," he said. "His head is bursting with plans for that mill. I saw him down there this morning when I was coming into work and he was skipping around the place looking as pleased as Punch. I never saw him like that before—I always thought he was a gloomy sort of a fellow. It just goes to show how a thing like good conditions of work can make the best of a man."

Miles agreed, but he reflected that the reason of Doyle's pleasure was probably Reid's death more than the happy prospects of his mill. He wondered again about Doyle, whether he were simple enough to murder a man one day and sing and whistle about his work the next, glad that a tiresome obstacle had been removed and careless of the method of its removal. Those brooding people often have a principle of cutting clean, and starting afresh, and turning over new leaves, because, fundamentally, they are never reconciled to imperfection. He hoped that Doyle's mind had not worked in this way, or presently he would have to find a new manager for his mill.

He felt refreshed from his talk with Wall, and in a more peaceful frame of mind he started to walk down the front avenue. He had no sooner rounded the first bend, so that the house was out of sight, than he became aware of the presence of Captain Merlin. He was walking in the park, keeping parallel with Miles, and giving a decided impression that he was stalking him. Miles thought that he looked more than half-cracked, sloping along in his badger-grey suit. He waved to him, and called out:

"Good morning, Merlin! Were you looking for me?"

Merlin came across to the fence and said crankily:

"I was, as a matter of fact, but there's no need to tell the world about it."

Miles raised his eyebrows, but said pleasantly:

"Come along out here, then, and we'll stroll along together."

He positively did not want Merlin in the house drinking whisky to-day. The Captain hesitated for a moment, while he looked up and down the avenue. Then he swung a surprisingly athletic leg over the fence and said:

"All right. Can't we go in? I have something private to say to you."

There was nothing to be done but to turn right around and bring him up to the house. Miles led him into the drawing-room, sat him down and poured him a glass of whisky with such firm decision that the Captain might have been forgiven for imagining that he was welcome to it. Once Miles had become resigned to being put upon, he had a special faculty for seeming to welcome the unwelcome. In this case his talent was wasted, for Merlin took a thirsty drink out of his glass quite unconcerned, looked about the room and said chattily:

"Damn nice place you have here."

"Yes," said Miles, noticing the involuntary claw-like movement of Merlin's free hand.

"You living here alone?"

"My cousin Germaine has very kindly come to housekeep for me," said Miles.

Merlin sat up straight. A splash of whisky shot out of his glass and fell on the arm of the chair. He rubbed it with his finger.

"What you need is a wife," he said abruptly.

"It's a bit late for that now," said Miles, amused. "I should have thought of it twenty years ago."

"I don't see anything funny about it," said Merlin sharply. "There's my daughter, Jane. You know her. Fine girl. Good housekeeper. Why don't you marry her?"

"Well, I hadn't thought—I mean, I don't know——"

"Must look after her, you know. Mother's dead, you see. She likes you. She told me."

"That was nice of her," said Miles gently. "But I don't know her very well, and I'm sure she has ideas of her own."

The man is mad, he was saying to himself. This is a crazy

140

conversation. He wished he could stop it, but he felt quite helpless, as he had felt before in the company of neurotics even of a milder sort than this. It was like standing under a waterfall, watching it roll down irrevocably. His heart ached for Jane. Merlin was saying:

"She's free to marry now, you know, Reid being dead." No emotion showed in his voice at the mention of his late son-in-law elect. "Never liked Reid much. Vulgar chap. Laughed too much. Noisy type—not quite a gentleman. Best I could do for her at the time, though. She'd get on better with you."

And my house is bigger, Miles thought cynically.

He jumped in his skin at Merlin's next remark:

"I'll tell her to come and see you, then, and that you're thinking of getting married."

"No, no! Don't do that!" Miles exclaimed in distress.

"Don't worry. She'll do what I say," said Merlin comfortably. "She always does. But you won't get her for nothing." He leaned back in a satisfied way as he said: "Reid gave me five hundred pounds."

Miles, who had been standing fidgeting about the cabinet of drinks, sat down suddenly on the nearest chair. His heart was pounding unpleasantly, and he had to stop and deliberately breathe deeply before he could manage to say:

"What are you suggesting?"

"Nothing to get excited about," said Merlin peevishly. "It's an old-fashioned way of doing things, but I don't see anything wrong with it."

Miles had often heard of the tendency of anxious parents to ensnare eligible bachelors for their daughters, but he had never imagined that they would set about it like this. One would think that Merlin was stalking an elephant. He would have given a great deal to have poured the remainder of Merlin's whisky over his head and kicked him out through the window. But there was Jane to think of. He would not for the world add to her torment in having such a father. She probably innocently

141

thought that with Reid out of the way, she would be free to marry Martin Doyle. Merlin was saying:

"You could make it seven hundred without any trouble, I'm sure. Or if that's not convenient you could give me five hundred now and we could have a gentlemen's agreement that I would get another two hundred later on."

"Gentlemen's agreement! My God!" exclaimed Miles involuntarily.

The Captain stood up, looking outraged, but keeping a tight hold on his glass.

"Are you suggesting that I am not a gentleman, Mr. de Cogan? I could call you out for that," he said menacingly.

"Call me out, indeed," thought Miles, his sense of humour coming to his rescue. "What century is he living in?"

He stretched out a hand and said:

"No offence meant, Merlin. I've been taken by surprise, that's all." Merlin nodded and they shook hands solemnly. "Do you mind if I take time to think it all over? I'm sure you will agree with me that one shouldn't rush into these things."

"Yes," said Merlin reluctantly. "Perhaps it's a new idea to you. I hope you're not a weakling. Took me only two days to make up my mind about Mrs. Merlin. I got her, all right. She only lived two years, though."

She was a wise judge, thought Miles. Something impelled him to ask:

"What do you think happened to Reid?"

"Don't know," said Merlin carelessly. "Often noticed how these big heavy chaps die suddenly."

But there was a certain smugness in his voice, and a gleam of self-satisfaction in his eye that sent a shivering idea into Miles's brain. Immediately his main concern was to get Merlin out of the house without further delay. He opened the door and stood waiting while Merlin put down his empty glass regretfully beside the decanter. Then they went out into the hall. He was glad that James appeared to open the front door, so that Merlin had to go away with a cryptic remark that he hoped to hear from Miles soon.

Back in the drawing-room Miles looked longingly at the whisky decanter, but he did not pour himself a drink. He felt that his brain needed all its natural powers unimpaired to deal with the idea that was coursing round and round inside it. He sat down in the chair that Merlin had used, but he felt distinctly uncomfortable in it and after a moment he moved to another one. For the first time in his life he appreciated the feelings of Father Bear in objecting to somebody sitting in his chair. The unpleasant aura of Merlin remained in the room, so that he could not endure it, and after a few minutes he got up restlessly and went outside again. He was overjoyed to see Inspector Henley coming slowly around by the side of the house.

"Thank Heaven you're back," he said in a low voice, and found himself clutching Henley's arm. "In another five minutes I'd have gone mad."

"What's the matter?" asked Henley sharply. "Has anything happened?"

"I think I know who killed Reid. He's just been here drinking my whisky. He's crazy."

"Come inside and tell me all about it," said Henley. "Try not to look so excited, please."

Miles found this rather difficult, but he succeeded in calming himself a little as he led Henley into the house. He avoided the front drawing-room, and they went into another room, called by tradition the Blue Room, at the back of the house. Soon, Miles thought grimly, he would have conceived a distaste for every room in his fine new house. What with Reid in the library and Merlin in the drawing-room. . . .

"Now, what's been happening?" Henley's impatient voice recalled him to his senses.

Miles told him almost word for word of his interview with Merlin, and the extraordinary proposition that had been put to him.

"And he told me that Reid had given him money—five hundred pounds—for his daughter already. The man is mad. How he could have thought I would listen to him——"

"Reid listened to him, apparently," said Henley mildly. "How do you conclude from this that he murdered Reid?"

"I should think it's obvious," said Miles, a little annoyed at his tale's cool reception. "Reid paid him for Jane. Then before they were married Merlin killed Reid. Now he sells her to me. Before I could marry her he would kill me. He could go on like that for ever, as far as I can see."

"As long as there were enough eligible bachelors left in the neighbourhood anyway," said Henley. "Don't think I'm not taking this seriously," he added quickly. "I agree with you that Merlin is mad, but my estimate of his character is different from yours. I've been visiting him this morning myself."

"So he must have come here straight from you."

"Yes, when I called the second time he had gone out. He encouraged me to go and arrest the manager of your mill, Martin Doyle. He regards him as definitely ineligible."

"Why don't you think that Merlin killed Reid so as to retain his saleable property?" Miles asked bluntly.

"It's hard to say," said Henley. "He's not a man of action. I think he is a man who would always see the possibilities of a situation, but who would not be able to bring about that situation. When he saw that Reid was attracted by Jane, he had no difficulty in seeing how this could profit himself. And when Reid was dead he saw your possibilities—or thought he did. He's an inveterate gambler, by the way. All those letters he writes are addressed to tipsters in England. This is private information, but it will give you an idea of why I have estimated his character as that of an opportunist rather than a practical man. Then he was expecting Reid to give Jane a valuable engagement ring, and he would hardly have killed him before she received it."

Miles nodded doubtfully, and Henley could see that he was

not convinced. He did not want Miles to go about proclaiming Merlin as the murderer of Reid, though he himself was by no means certain of his innocence. The question of the presentation of the ring was nothing, for instance, to the prospect of Jane's inheriting Reid's money and property. Indeed, if that will had been signed, Jane would have got the ring too. He knew now what it was that Merlin had been planning this morning, and he congratulated himself on having been right in his guess that the Captain was up to something. But he was long enough in the world to know that no one ever completely understands or properly estimates the character of another. And his many guesses at Merlin's character were worthless from the point of view of evidence.

"What did you answer to Merlin's proposal?" he asked.

"Oh, I said it was all so sudden," said Miles, with a little characteristic gesture of his hands. "I said I needed time to think it over."

"Good. Keep him on a string. That's the way to get more out of him," said Pat approvingly.

"But I don't like it," Miles said. "I don't want that fellow around the place any more."

"The next time he comes, I'll talk to him," said Henley. "I have a piece of news for him anyway. By the way, if it's any comfort to you, I don't think that Merlin would want to murder you."

"That is indeed a comfort," murmured Miles. "I hope you have a good reason for saying so."

It was not yet midday, and Henley felt that he would have time for an interview with Martin Doyle before lunch. He felt sorry for Miles, and very much regretted having to leave him, but time was too valuable to be spent in consoling him. The eager way in which Miles walked to the door with him betrayed his distaste for being left alone. On the front steps Pat relented and said:

"Would you have time to walk down to the mill with me? You could explain my position to Martin Doyle."

15

As they walked along the back avenue Miles said:

"You know Doyle already, I think?"

"Oh, yes. I've met him several times when I was here before. You're lucky to have him, you know. He's a man of ideas."

"I'm glad you agree with me about that," said Miles eagerly. "I thought him a fine person. A bit gloomy and frustrated, but nothing that won't cure with marriage and pleasanter working conditions."

He gave Henley a short description of the plan for the development of the mill.

"If I didn't do something of the sort I'd feel like a parasite," he said. "It would be criminal to waste a good man like Doyle. And I'd like to see if a lively industry of this kind would put the village on its feet. Strange thing, when I was coming here, Barne advised me to sell the mill. He thought there was no future in it."

Henley said that he had always thought it strange that the mill had not been developed.

"The old man didn't believe in industries, as far as I can make out," said Miles. "He thought that the estate was the important thing. I rather think he didn't want to mop up all the potential servants in the village, but perhaps I'm being too hard on him there. Did you know him?"

"Not personally," said Pat with a smile. "He would not have known me except as his good man, so I need hardly say that I kept out of his way. The village people liked him, though he was rather limited from their point of view. He was old

146

enough to get away with the grand manner—they would never have tolerated it from a younger man."

At the gate they saw Dr. Donovan's car coming towards them. It pulled up, and the doctor's head came out of the window.

"I've just heard the news from Lawlor," he said to Henley. "You're going to have a nice time finding out how Reid drank that stuff."

Henley made a warning gesture behind Miles's back. Donovan raised his eyebrows, but said no more about the poison. Henley made a mental note to warn him again not to mention it, for he had an instinctive objection to handing out information unnecessarily. The inquest would reveal everything, but until then he preferred some measure of secrecy.

"Paul Walsh appears to have something to say to you," Donovan said. "Fellow has a mind like a lame kangaroo."

"How so?" said Miles, pleased at this simile.

"Slow on the jump," said Donovan. "He works around to things gradually. I was talking to him just now, and he was wondering whether you would laugh at a suggestion he had. I assured him that the Guards never laugh while they are investigating a murder."

"Thank you," said Henley. "I'll see him later on."

With a cheerful wave the doctor drove off. Miles said doubtfully:

"I suppose sudden death means nothing to a doctor."

"Doctors are human too," said Henley. "Donovan is not very sorry about Reid's end."

"Reid tried to injure him in his profession," said Miles. "He told me so himself. He took it good-humouredly enough, but it's easy to understand why he's not heart-broken after Reid. Donovan said that Reid used to tell the County people—his best patients—that he was no good. He could have ruined his practice—it's the easiest thing in the world to damage a doctor's reputation."

"What happened?"

"No one believed Reid, Donovan says," said Miles. "Still, he must have been very uneasy. It could very soon become the habit of the people here to run into Dublin every time they want to see a doctor."

Methodically, Henley considered Donovan as a suspect. But enormously in his favour there was the fact that he could have given a death certificate for Reid, and boxed him up and had him buried, and no more need have been said. Instead he had elected to call the Guards. Henley sighed. In no time, it seemed, he would be considering the parish priest as a possible murderer. He hoped that Donovan would never realize that he had been the subject of even five minutes' suspicion.

The entrance to the mill itself was through a wide arched doorway of a great age. The walls and floor were powdered finely with flour, and they picked their way across to the door of a little office at the back. Henley wished that Miles were not with him, for he would not mention Jane Merlin until he and Doyle were alone. Now he would have to confine his inquiries to the agitation against Reid's road-house, which he had begun to regard as a minor though disgraceful episode.

Doyle had been sitting at his desk in the office when they arrived. He saw them through the glass panels and jumped up to open the door. For a moment he looked uneasy and then he said:

"Good morning, Mr. de Cogan. Good morning, Henley. Glad to see you again."

They shook hands and he made them sit down, crowding the tiny room. Henley said:

"I'm here on business this time—we think Reid was poisoned, you know."

"I had heard that," said Doyle.

"It's a bad thing to have happened," said Pat. "All these meetings must have preyed on his mind."

"No doubt," said Doyle coolly. "I should have thought he was tougher than that."

148

"You took a hand in the meetings yourself, I hear," said Pat gently.

"A small part," said Doyle. "I wasn't very much interested in whether he built a road-house or not."

This was the exact truth, as Henley knew. Being an educated man, Doyle was not likely to reveal his true feelings about Reid unasked, particularly as they were irrelevant to the line that Henley affected to be investigating. But Henley knew that Doyle must be regarded as capable of murder. He was a practical man, a man who was capable of making a firm decision and carrying it through. He was a scientific man, too, who would attend meticulously to each detail in turn. And he had an overpowering reason for wanting to be rid of Reid, whom he must have seen as the instrument of Jane Merlin's torment.

"You wrote a letter to Reid, I think?" he said.

"The committee composed the letter," said Doyle. "I only joined in that for the fun of it. None of it was really serious."

"Not the piece about the pigs? Nor the rabbit's blood on the foot of the letter?"

Doyle raised his eyebrows.

"So you've heard all about those things," he said.

"They were serious enough," Henley pointed out. "The blood undoubtedly constituted a threat to his person, and the pigs were to injure his property. That's serious enough, in all conscience."

Doyle looked uncomfortable.

"The pigs were never let into his garden," he said, still trying to make the whole affair look like a joke.

"Reid was dead before the appointed time," Henley said quietly.

"You don't think we killed him to stop him from building a pub at the cross-roads, do you?"

"No. But almost every person connected with those meetings had something personal against Reid."

Miles had listened to all this in a state of acute discomfort. At any moment, he thought, Henley was going to accuse Doyle of having murdered Reid. The room felt unbearably small and hot and the machinery of the mill seemed suddenly to have grown louder. Henley was saying smoothly:

"You know more about that side of the business than I do. If you could think it over and tell me about each of the people, it would be a great help. I'm not asking you to accuse them of anything—just tell me if you know in what way they were connected with Reid."

"I'd rather not, thanks," said Doyle shortly.

"Just as you please," said Henley. "I'll be able to find out elsewhere."

Miles stood up.

"I'll just continue my walk," he said trying to sound unconcerned. "I'll see you at lunch, Henley."

The others stood up too, and Henley opened the door for him. But Martin Doyle seemed not to see him at all. His hands were twitching among the papers on his desk and it was obvious that he was quite unable to answer Miles's word of farewell. In the doorway Miles paused and said:

"You don't have to answer any questions without consulting a solicitor. Shall I send Barne down to you? He's staying at my place."

Doyle's expression softened a little as he said:

"No, thank you. I'll be careful."

Henley said:

"I'll warn him in time if I think he should consult a solicitor. I don't think there is any need for that at present."

Miles could see that Henley was angry with him for interfering, but he could not have stood by and seen Doyle tricked into a false position. Henley was a very pleasant fellow, to be sure, and the son of an old friend, but a policeman is trained to suppress his human quality of pity, Miles thought, so that ordinary people can never really trust him. Miles looked back once after the door had clicked shut behind him, and saw the two men sit down again, slowly and watchfully.

The little interruption had obviously given Doyle time to see the implication of Henley's statement that everyone who had taken part in the agitation had some personal grievance against Reid. Henley had made it plain that he was not excluding Doyle from this indictment. It seemed that it had come as a shock to Doyle to discover that the fact of his personal grievance against Reid was known. This did not surprise Henley. He was always encountering people who imagined that their private lives were secret, and who were horrified to find how little, even of their thoughts, they had managed to conceal. Miles had been unjust to him in imagining him as devoid of pity. In fact, Pat had more than his share of this inconvenient quality, and it hampered and depressed him daily in the course of his work. He made an effort to put Doyle at his ease again by using a conversational tone to say:

"No one could get as excited about the moral effect of Reid's road-house as this village appeared to do. Anyone could see that there were other reasons there too. Did you see how the people reacted to the news of Reid's death?"

"No. But I heard about it."

"What did you think of it?"

Doyle shrugged and said:

"Guilty consciences, I suppose."

"And suspicious of each other," said Pat. "They felt that someone had gone too far. But I think that someone used the situation to cover his tracks, hoping that Reid's death would look like suicide." Doyle looked at him blankly and silently. "You had a letter from Reid on the morning of the day he died. What was in that letter?"

Doyle said:

"Who said I had a letter from Reid?"

"Joe Connolly, the barman," said Pat patiently. "He didn't seem to think there was any secret in it. He understood that it

151

was an answer to your threatening letter with the rabbit's blood. I should like to see that letter."

"I burnt it," said Doyle shortly.

"That's a pity. Joe said you did not show the letter to the committee because there were personal things in it, but that you told them to let the pigs into Reid's garden as arranged."

"You know a lot," said Doyle sourly.

"I've been asking a few questions," said Henley. "If people don't answer I get suspicious."

"Joe was very open with you, at any rate," said Doyle angrily. "Did he mention that he was the ringleader and chief speech-maker of the whole agitation? Was he so busy turning your suspicions on me that he forgot to mention his daughter Nora?"

"He did mention her," said Pat, "and he expressed the greatest satisfaction at Reid's death."

"Then why not go and annoy him instead of me?"

"I intend to," said Pat. "What was in Reid's letter that you burnt?"

There was a pause in which Henley got out a cigarette and lit it. An angry gesture of refusal was all Doyle's answer to his offer of one. Presently Doyle said:

"I see I'll have to tell you about that letter, or you'll imagine all sorts of things about it. You'll certainly never hit on the truth. You know that Miss Merlin was said to be about to marry Reid?"

"Yes," said Pat gently, admiring Doyle's choice of words. "I was talking to her father this morning."

"Her father!" Doyle snorted. "That man is a devil. It was all his idea. She didn't want to marry Reid at all—hated him, in fact."

"Yes; I was talking to Miss Merlin too."

"Did she tell you that?" asked Doyle in surprise.

"It came out in the conversation," said Pat vaguely.

"Perhaps you know, too, that Captain Merlin has taken money from Reid?"

152

Henley nodded, and Doyle looked disappointed for a moment. Then he said:

"In that case, you know most of the story. Jane and I have been friendly for some time, but when her father told her that he had taken money from Reid, she imagined that it was up to her to honour the bargain by marrying him. I had endless arguments with her about it." Drops of sweat appeared on his forehead at the recollection of those conversations. "Always she would agree that it was nonsense to fall in with the wishes of such a crazy old coot as her father, especially in a thing that only concerned herself. She'd leave me determined to go home and tell the old man to go to Jericho, and then the next time I'd meet her she'd be as bad as ever. What I could not contend with was the constant nagging that she had to put up with at home. He was always able to wear her down. She was going mad before my very eyes."

He choked back an anguished sob. Henley said nothing at all. Doyle folded his hands together on the desk, and they clutched each other until the knuckles whitened. After a moment he said:

"The old man had asked me for money. Perhaps I would have given it to him if I had had it, but I have nothing but my job. He knew that, of course. I told him one or two things about himself, which was unwise, I suppose. But I couldn't bear his smug face and his talk about good old-fashioned methods."

"And the letter," Henley reminded him.

"Yes, I'm coming to that. I had to tell you the rest of it so that you'd understand about Reid. He had everything that I wanted," Doyle explained painfully. "He was—very attached —to Jane—and he was going to marry her. I couldn't bear that. Somehow he knew that I was mixed up in writing the letter about the road-house, because he sent the answer to me. It said something like this: 'Dear Doyle. Never mind about the old road-house. I don't care a damn about it really, though I'm not going to be bullied by the—he used a nasty word there—of

153

Dangan. Come over to my side and we'll do business together. If you'll stop the meetings I'll give you my interest in Miss Merlin, and we'll start off fresh. You'll see I'll make your fortune.' It went something like that. I couldn't understand what he was getting at. There was something about being very fond of Miss Merlin but fonder still of the mill. That drove me wild. I told the men to send the pigs into his place that night. I was sorry he was dead before it could be done."

He stopped suddenly. Henley gave him a long, searching look. The sincerity of his last remark could not be doubted; nor the savage frustration in his tone of voice. If this were not a fine piece of acting, surely it meant that Doyle was not Reid's murderer. But again he reminded himself that Doyle was an educated, sophisticated man, and that he was as well able to assess the effect of his words as was Henley himself.

Promising himself that he would have further conversation with Doyle later, Henley stood up to go. The two men looked at each other across the desk, but there was nothing to be said. They had been friends before, and perhaps they would be friends again, but a great many things would have to change before that would be possible. At last Henley dropped his eyes. He went quickly out of the office and out of the mill through the floury archway, feeling as he went the penetrating eyes of half a dozen workmen on his back. He would have given a great deal to have known what they were thinking.

16

Feeling that he needed the moral support of his own kind, Henley went in search of Lawlor. As he walked through the village it seemed to him that people were going about their business with a studied air of righteousness, as if they hoped that their straight backs and large shopping baskets and flocks of attendant children would go to prove that they were incapable of anything as nasty as murder.

Lawlor was at the barracks in the village, overflowing off a very inadequate stool at the table in the day-room. He asked Pat to sit down, and looked with disgust at the old kitchen chair which was all he had to offer him.

"Never mind," said Pat. "When you come to visit me I'll have the same for you. What's the news of Reid's activities yesterday?"

"Mighty little," said the sergeant heavily. "He spent the morning working at home. His Maggie had asked for the evening off to go to Dublin. She had arranged it about a fortnight ago. She went on the bus at two o'clock. She left a cold meal for him in the dining-room, cold chicken and trout in aspic and salad and I don't know what. Enough to make your mouth water. Georgie Fahy would have made coffee for him at about seven, and he would have polished off the whole lot at one go. He always had a powerful stroke, they said."

"Coffee?" said Henley.

"Yes. He preferred tea, Georgie said, but he knew that coffee was a gentleman's drink."

"That's the first I heard about a meal," said Henley heatedly.

155

"There was no sign of it in the dining-room this morning. I was in there, wasn't I? I didn't see any food——"

"Easy on, sir," said Lawlor. "I know what it feels like. It was only after you were gone this morning that I got it out of them. Madame Maggie set to last night and cleared away the whole lot. An old segoshioner of hers came visiting her about nine o'clock, and the two ladies sat down, one on each side of the kitchen table and perished every ounce of the grub. They wouldn't give Georgie any, or I'd say he'd have helped."

"And how are they feeling this morning?" asked Pat.

"Fresh and well," said Lawlor gloomily, "as you saw. There was nothing the matter with that food, I'm sure, though it would take a powerful lot of poison to finish off Maggie."

"Who was the segoshioner?" Henley asked solemnly.

"Mrs. Hooper. A widow-woman. Her sister has the post office. She used to be housekeeper above in the big house, but Mr. de Cogan gave her the push. She was a great hanger-on of Mr. Reid's for some reason."

"Was Georgie about Reid's place yesterday afternoon?"

"Yes, but he was in the garden most of the time, or around by the garage. He doesn't know when Reid went out, so he's not much use."

"I'll have another talk with him later," said Henley. "He seemed an observant sort of a chap."

The sergeant was shaking his big head.

"What do you think of the two old lassies wiring into Reid's supper and they knowing he was dead only a couple of hours? I asked them how they could bring themselves to do it, and they said that waste was a sin. Oh, they're a well-matched pair of jades, them two," said Lawlor, his grammar deserting him in the depth of his emotion.

"So Reid didn't go down to the hotel for a drink, or visit Captain Merlin or anyone else——" Henley was meditating.

"Not that we can find out," said Lawlor. "He could have slipped into Merlin's without any trouble, only that Georgie

Fahy might have seen him on the avenue, or Merlin could have slipped into him. I'm inclined to think that someone visited him, for he was a great man to pour a drink for a visitor. He couldn't have anyone in the house more than five minutes without offering them whisky or gin, and he even used to keep syphons of lemonade for the ladies. Always trying to keep his end up, you know, showing that he could afford it."

"Would he have offered a drink to Joe Connolly, if he had called?" asked Henley softly.

Lawlor cocked an eye at him.

"I think not," he said. "If Joe wanted to poison him, he would have had to get him in the hotel bar. Reid was so particular about being a gentleman that I doubt if he could have sat down to a drink with any working man."

But if he had wanted to make friends with Joe again after the unpleasant scene in the bar, he might have unbent enough to offer him a drink, thought Henley.

"Was there any sign that someone had had a drink with Reid in the afternoon?" he asked.

"I'm afraid I fell down on it there," said Lawlor apologetically. "When I heard about them clearing away the meal, I'm afraid I—I shouted at Maggie. That's a thing a big fellow like me should never do. I frightened the heart in her, and she could hardly tell you how many feet she had under her in the end."

Henley would have given much to have seen the massive, placid Lawlor run amok. He said gently:

"I'll see her myself again, and she might remember something."

He told Lawlor about his interview with Doyle.

"Reid and Merlin were a nice pair of rats," said Lawlor with feeling. "No wonder the poor little girl was nearly off her head between the two of them."

"But the trouble is that I don't know if Doyle told the whole truth about that letter," said Henley. "For all I know, Reid may have finished the letter by asking Doyle to come and visit him in the afternoon so that they could talk over whatever he had in mind about the mill."

"Doyle is a black little lad, all right," said Lawlor. "And then what about Mr. de Cogan? What brought Reid visiting him on the night before he died, and why didn't he tell us about that? There's a short cut across de Cogan's park nearly to Reid's front door, and he could easily have come around that way. He'd have a good chance of no one seeing him cross the road. There's gallons of nicotine in Dangan, with all the roses."

"But he had no reason to kill Reid," Henley protested. "Why, he hardly knew him!"

"Someone killed him," said Lawlor simply.

Henley got up and walked over to the window. He had yet to find a plausible reason for the murder of Reid among the people connected with him. Until he had heard the contents of Reid's letter to Doyle, it had seemed to him that Jane Merlin had had a good reason. Jane had unconsciously confirmed this by saying that Reid had cooled a little towards her lately, and had even refrained from giving her the engagement ring. It certainly looked as if Reid had been in the process of changing his mind, and if this were happening she would have no further need to murder him. On the other hand, it was possible that she had not known that the need for killing Reid was gone. As for her father, it remained to be seen how he would receive the news of the unsigned will.

Doyle's motive had been strong, but it also would have disappeared with Jane Merlin's. Then, if the contents of the letter had been as he had said, it seemed that Reid wanted some kind of co-operation with him over the mill. Reid had had nothing to do with Doyle until now, so it was hard to imagine what it was that he had wanted. Perhaps he had been about to offer him a job in one of the factories of which he was a Director. The vagueness of this part of the business was infuriating. At first he had been quite confident that he would soon find the murderer of such a universally disliked man. Now he heartily wished that Reid had been loved by all, so that one person who hated him could be identified at a glance.

He turned back to Lawlor.

"Paul Walsh has something on his mind, it seems," he said. "I've reached such a dead end that I think I'll go and have a chat with him. He can hardly make things worse than they are."

Lawlor sighed as he reached for an official pen and grasped it awkwardly in his colossal hand.

"Fine for you, sir," he said. "I'd rather be doing that than making out a report. The first day that fellow Reid set foot in Dangan I knew he'd be a heart-scald. Before he came we had nothing but lost dogs and fishing licences and extra ration cards and that class of thing——"

He shook his head gloomily. Henley went out and left him to it.

It was only a step across the road to the hotel, and he was still chuckling over Lawlor's line of reasoning as he stepped into the hall. There was no one about except a work-weary black cocker spaniel asleep at the foot of the stairs. Henley put his head into the bar, but found it deserted. Then a few half-hearted taps on a typewriter sounded from the office on the other side of the hall. He went over and opened the door. Paul Walsh was there, poking at an aged typewriter with two inexpert forefingers.

"I'm very glad to be interrupted, Henley," he said, as he got up. "I'm no good at this kind of thing." He looked with dislike around the gloomy little office. "Let's not sit here," he said. "Horrible little hole."

As they came out into the hall Henley said mildly:

"Why don't you clean it up?"

"Why should I?" said Walsh, staring. "The customers never go in there."

There was no more to be said, for there spoke the voice of

159

several generations of hotel-keepers. They went upstairs to a lounge at the front of the hotel, where varnished stout fish lay in glass cases around the walls, alternating with stuffed, beady-eyed wildfowl and unlikely looking shells. Here and there hung framed facetious verses about fishing. The windows were open so that the soft sunny air, hay-scented, was all around them.

"Dr. Donovan told me that you had something to tell me," said Henley without preamble.

Paul Walsh's brow became furrowed and an earnest look came into his brown eyes, so that Pat knew he was about to think. He appreciated the tremendous effort being made on his behalf while he waited impatiently for the results. Presently Walsh said:

"I didn't know whether you would like to hear it. It's nothing really. I just thought you might be having trouble working it all out, you know."

"I am having trouble," said Pat. "I shall be glad if you can help me in any way."

"Oh, I don't know if it will be any help," said Walsh with maddening diffidence. There was a pause before he went on:

"Do you remember last night when we found Joe doped in the bar?" Pat nodded. "Well, after you had gone I was talking to him for a while, just to soothe him down. He told me that you had questioned him about the meetings and who had been at them and so on. He mentioned Mrs. Hooper, and I got thinking about her. I hope you won't laugh?"

"I won't laugh," said Pat, and he meant it.

"Mrs. Hooper and Reid were great friends. But she was at the meetings, and I just wondered why. That's all, really."

Henley observed Walsh with respect while he thanked him sincerely for this hint. It was early yet, and he had had plenty of reason for his investigations in other directions, but he wondered how long it would have taken him to get around to Mrs. Hooper. Walsh, whose thought processes obviously gave him pain, had noticed the incongruity of her position. Still, he

160

reminded himself, it was far too soon to be elated. He had yet to see Mrs. Hooper and make her talk. He could have embraced Paul Walsh for showing him the way to his next line of inquiry just at the moment when he most needed it. Walsh protested in embarrassment that he was not at all clever, really, that he just knew the village people well. And inevitably he began to have qualms about setting the police on Mrs. Hooper.

"She's a poor widow, you know," he said. "It's a shame to make you suspicious of her. I never meant to say that she had anything to do with Reid's death——"

"Never mind, old man," said Pat. "I'm suspicious of everyone anyway—even of yourself, if it comes to that."

The surprise of this struck Walsh dumb and motionless, and with another word of thanks Pat left him sitting among his furred and finny friends and went downstairs.

He knew where Mrs. Hooper lived. Someone had told him that she was at the post office with her sister, Miss Byrne. The post office was four doors down the street and in a matter of seconds he was standing at its little stained counter. Aged brass bars made it impossible for him to make a grab at Miss Byrne, even if he had felt so inclined. The walls were distempered with the shade of green most favoured by the Board of Works, and chatty notices about weed-killers and wireless licences and old-age pensions and saving certificates were pasted here and there.

In the leisurely manner of all postmistresses, Miss Byrne dragged herself away from the forms that she had been stamping and came over to glare through the bars at him like a black leopard. The main difference was that her face was yellow. After she had snarled: "Well?" Pat comforted himself with the reflection that she was probably consumed with some inward, venomous complaint. He said that he wished to speak to Mrs. Hooper.

"You're the Guards, aren't you?" she snapped.

"That's right," said Pat. "I'm the Guards."

"You'd better come in. She's within."

She opened a little door under the counter so that he could crawl through. Then she opened another door behind her and jerked her head to indicate that he could go inside. He did so, feeling that if this were an Edgar Wallace novel he would immediately be set upon by little Chinamen and dropped through a waiting trapdoor, bound hand and foot, into the Thames. However, the Thames was a comforting distance away, and the little kitchen in which he found himself was not at all terrifying. Its only occupant was Mrs. Hooper, who was engaged in cooking dinner on the range.

She turned to stare, with a long spoon in her hand—like someone about to sup with the devil. The range was fiercely hot and several pots were sending up clouds of steam, so that in the first minute Pat felt the sweat come out on his forehead. Mrs. Hooper was like her sister in appearance, and Pat looked at her almost with affection as she stood there glaring at him. He knew how to handle her kind.

"I want a few words with you," he said sharply. "The cooking can wait. Sit down, please!"

He had no intention of allowing her to put him off by prodding at her pots while he was talking. He placed her at the kitchen table which stood under the window. Then he threw up the bottom of the window so that they should not stifle, and stood threateningly before her. Just as he was about to start thundering at her, a magnificent marmalade cat jumped on to the window-sill from the little yard outside, stepped delicately on to the table, and from there to Mrs. Hooper's lap, where it settled in a purring heap. Her fingers trembled a little as she fondled its ears. Pat made a hopeless little gesture with his hand as he watched her. It was no use his ever trying to act the bully, he thought in annoyance. Something would always happen to soften him before he could even begin. He pulled out a chair from the table and sat down. The only intimidating machinery that he allowed himself was his notebook, which he placed open before him.

"I want to hear about your friendship with Mr. Reid," he said gently.

"Why should I tell you? How do I know what use you'll make of what I say?" she said sourly.

"I've heard that you used to be friendly with Mr. Reid," said Pat, "but on the evening that he died you celebrated by eating the very supper that he would have taken. That looks bad, you must admit."

"I don't admit anything." She stopped for a moment and then said in a slightly pleasanter tone: "What do you want to know?"

"You are a widow, I think. Where did you live until you came to Dangan?"

"We lived in County Limerick." She named Reid's village. "My husband was a milesman on the railway."

"Was that where you met Mr. Reid?"

"Yes. I knew him since he was a little boy. His father was the blacksmith." She smiled sourly. "When my husband died, he got me the job with Sir Miles."

Pat made a note or two and laid down his pencil. He wished he had known Reid better when he was alive. Then perhaps he would have understood what lay behind Mrs. Hooper's association with him. Had he helped her to become Sir Miles's housekeeper out of nostalgic charity towards an old friend and neighbour, or had he done it as the price of her keeping silence about his origins? If the latter were the reason, it seemed likely that she had failed to honour the bargain. Certainly it was common knowledge in the village that his father had been a blacksmith, and who was better qualified to supply this information than Mrs. Hooper?

"Then Mr. Reid was friendly with Sir Miles?" he said.

"He had influence with him," she said. "He got me the job there, and I did it well. But I got no thanks from Mr. de Cogan —I was turned out without a moment's notice. But that's what you learn to expect in this world."

Henley was surprised at this. He would not have thought that Miles would be so hard-hearted. "Didn't you say anything to Mr. de Cogan? Did you just go without a word?" he asked.

Immediately she became flustered and uneasy. She clutched a handful of the cat, which gave a low growl and whacked at her hand with a soft paw. She stroked it absently and presently it began to purr again.

"You've been talking to Mr. de Cogan," she said at last, while Henley waited, holding his breath. "I got carried away, I didn't mean any of it. He said he wouldn't hold it against me —he's a decent man. He is giving me a pension of five pounds a month, though I only worked in the place a couple of years." She stopped, and looked up at him. "How well you can come after me, because I'm a poor woman. Why don't you get after the last housekeeper that was there, and ask her why she was thrown out on her ear? Ask her that, and you'll get a surprise." She snorted venomously. "Yes, and she wasn't long getting herself back in again, and the poor innocent that's there couldn't see through her."

"Are you talking about Miss Germaine de Cogan?"

"Who else? Oh, she's a smart one. But I know all about her, and some of it she wouldn't like Mr. Miles to hear, too. She's nicely fixed now, back in the big house, and her friend in the lodge, Miss Hearn, and between the pair of them they'll suck the blood out of the poor unfortunate man."

"What are you talking about? Tell me more about them," said Henley hopefully, but she would not.

"I'm not going to be mixed up in anything nasty," she said with delightful irony. "I've suffered enough. I was that distracted, I went to Mr. Reid and told him what happened. He said he'd get me back into my job again. But he never did anything, only all smooth talk and what a great fellow he was and how he knew everyone. So when the meetings were going on I joined in—not at first, but towards the end, when I was sure he was doing nothing for me."

So that was the explanation of Mrs. Hooper, and a very simple, ordinary explanation it was. Having once profited by Reid's help, she now felt that she had a right to it. It was amusing to think with what wicked speed she had gone to Reid's house and helped Maggie to eat his supper.

He was not disappointed in Mrs. Hooper after all. He would have to find out more about her, of course, for it was possible that she had poisoned Reid herself. She had the entrée to his house, and it was more than likely that he would have had a conciliatory drink with her. Her motive would have been miserably weak in a normal person, but he thought it possible that she was capable of poisoning him just to show him that he could not let her down so easily. He was convinced that she had something on her conscience. The trouble with a woman of her years was that it was hard to distinguish the conscience from the imagination. He determined to question Miles further about the conversation during which he had dismissed her. And something she had said had started a small but very clear line of thought working within him, so that he was able to thank her for her kind help with genuine sincerity before he left her.

She looked at him as if she thought he were mad. At the door he looked back to see her still sitting there, stroking the cat, while her pots boiled over and sizzled on the range.

17

Henley would have been only a little late for lunch, but he deliberately sneaked upstairs to his room and did not come down until everyone else had finished. He could not bear to sit and chat with Miles and Germaine and Barne, and he almost wished that he had stayed in official mystery at the hotel. He had no doubt that the party in the dining-room was pleased at his absence. No one likes a bloodhound sniffing around his feet at meal-time.

In fact, however, Miles was sorry that Henley was not present, for he guessed why he had not come in. There was no conversation during the meal, and Mr. Barne's appreciation of the asparagus and Hollandaise sauce was all too audible. He made little smacking noises over his coffee, too, and then disappeared into the office again. Miles arranged with James to give him his tea there at four o'clock, saying that he seemed very busy and that it would save him the trouble of coming to the drawing-room.

After James had gone they sat on for a while. Germaine said:

"You've made a tremendous hit with the village people. Julia tells me they're all talking about the mill and the good times that are coming."

"What do you think of it?" Miles asked, for the first time.

"It's a wonderful thing for them," she said. "Something of the sort should have been done years ago. People are afraid to make a beginning, afraid that it won't work out as they had planned it, or that they won't get complete agreement on details from the other people concerned."

"I'm prepared for that," said Miles, "and I don't care. The

sooner they take over the whole thing themselves the better I'll like it."

"Have you discussed it with Mr. Barne?" she asked.

"I haven't had a chance," said Miles. "I wrote to him for a draft agreement, but he has not yet said anything to me about it. I'm looking forward to hearing what he thinks of the plan. He knows the village and the people so well that I'm sure he'll have plenty of good advice for me. I'm going to need good advice in an undertaking like this."

He stood up saying:

"I think I'll go at once."

Inspector Henley, coming down the stairs, saw Miles cross the hall to the office. He waited until Miles had opened the door and gone inside before he came on down to the hall. He looked hopefully into the dining-room where he was pleased to see James still clearing away plates and glasses. James hurried to lay a place for him and went in search of food.

"There's ham, sir, I know, and we'll have a salad for you in two shakes," he said as he shot through the door.

A minute later Germaine came into the room saying:

"James told me you were here. What a pity you couldn't get back in time. We had a very nice lunch. Now you'll have to do with something cold, I'm afraid."

"That will be delightful," said Henley, somewhat uncomfortably, for he had a strong impression that she knew he had spent the last hour lurking upstairs. He wished that James had had the wit to keep his presence secret.

Looking at Germaine's pleasant, rather absent-minded face, he wondered what it was that Mrs. Hooper had been hinting about her. He dreaded the task of questioning her, as he always dreaded these blank gentlewomen. They were like cotton-wool—soft and clean-looking and very tough. They were often just a little bit queer in the head, in his experience, but it was hard to detect this because they had been taught from a very early age to hide it. They had a real knack of keeping their business to themselves, and if Germaine ran true to her type, it was highly unlikely that she would unwittingly give anything away.

All the time she stayed with him, while he ate the meal that James provided, he found himself piling question on question in his own mind about her association with the murder of Reid. Mrs. Hooper's hints had only served to remind him of what he had known already. The village of Dangan had rocked when Germaine had left the house in which she had been brought up and had gone to live in the lodge which had hitherto been inhabited only by gardeners. Everyone knew that she had fallen out with her brother, and every kind of speculation had been made as to the cause of the quarrel. But never the smallest hint of a reason had leaked out. When Mrs. Hooper had gone to work at the house, she had suddenly found herself overwhelmed with invitations to tea in the village. But she had never had anything really satisfactory to report, and after one or two obvious and unsuccessful prevarications, she had adopted Germaine's own aloof manner and had become an unapproachable *grande dame* in her own right.

Now the reason of that quarrel had become very important. It seemed to Henley quite possible that Reid had known something about it. If he was friendly enough with Sir Miles to be able to get Mrs. Hooper into Dangan House as housekeeper, it was likely enough that Sir Miles had confided some of the details of the quarrel to him. Surely Sir Miles was human enough to need someone to whom he could complain about his sister. Supposing that they had quarrelled over something that was discreditable to Germaine. If Reid had threatened to tell Sir Miles's heir about it, so that Germaine would be asked to leave again and Mrs. Hooper would be brought back—there was a reason why Germaine might have thought it necessary to poison Reid. Reid had assured Mrs. Hooper that he would be able to help her. She thought he had forgotten about her, but it was equally possible that he was watching for a suitable moment to approach Miles. And he had done so! On the very evening before his death, Georgie Fahy had seen him come out of Miles's gate.

Pat waited for a break in Germaine's discourse on tulips and said:

"Is Mr. de Cogan about the place?"

"He's talking to Mr. Barne," she said, with a quizzical look. "I could fetch him out for you, if you like. They are in the office."

"No, no! Sorry if I'm preoccupied," he mumbled. "So many things to think of, you know."

If Miles did not know why Germaine and her brother had quarrelled, or if he refused to discuss it, where could he turn for the answer? He could let Sergeant Lawlor loose on Mrs. Hooper, perhaps. Lawlor would not be put off by cats or poor widows or pathetic little kitchens. There was John Wall, too, who had known Sir Miles very well. He might have had a hint at the nature of the quarrel. Of one thing he was certain, that he would not ask Germaine herself about it unless he had concrete proof that it had something to do with the case. She was far too intelligent to tell him what he wanted to know without any reason adduced. Later he might be forced to try this as a last resort, but he hoped that it would not be necessary.

Suddenly he thought of the Hearns. Julia and Germaine had been bosom friends for years, and it was not likely that Julia would be disposed to gossip about her friend. But old Mrs. Hearn was quite another story. He stood up and folded his napkin carefully as he said:

"I'll see Mr. de Cogan later on—perhaps at tea-time."

He promised himself that he would see Mr. Barne, too, if he could divert him from his work for a little while. Even such a dried-up little stick as he was might have been Sir Miles's confidant. Sometimes such people are chosen because no one can conceive of their taking a personal interest in the secret confided. And he could expect co-operation from Barne, thank heaven, for he was the only friend that Reid had had. Somewhere inside the little lawyer there was a spark of indignation at the coldness with which everyone viewed Reid's death. He had been asking about when the funeral would be, Henley remembered. None of the others had expressed the smallest interest in what became of Reid's remains.

He escorted Germaine back to the drawing-room, and left her there, trying to cover his eagerness to be gone. As he started down the drive he was aware that she was watching him from the window.

In the bright little garden in front of the lodge, the massive Julia was weeding the flower-beds. She looked up as Henley came in through the gate, and then straightened.

"Good afternoon, Miss Hearn," he said. "Could I have a word with your mother, I wonder?"

She looked surprised, and not very pleased. On her large face every emotion showed with double intensity. She was like a whale, he thought—or rather, a shark, with those big teeth.

"You know my mother is almost completely bedridden now," she said. "She gets up in the evenings sometimes, but not every day."

"Can I not see her then?"

"Oh, yes. You can see her. I'll bring you up to her room."

She hesitated for a moment and then said: "Are you just paying a call, or is it something to do with Reid's death?"

Her bland eye gave no hint of any sardonic intention in the first part of her question, but he knew that she remembered that he had had no particular friendship with her mother.

"I just want some local history—old stuff that she might know," he said. "Reid was your landlord, before you came here, I think?"

"Yes. But he was no great friend of mother's. She was rather inclined to keep him in his place, poor fellow."

She would be, Henley thought, as he waited in the little sitting-room while Julia went upstairs to warn her mother of his coming. A sour old thing, Mrs. Hearn had been before she had become so helpless. He doubted if her character would have improved since last he had met her.

Presently he was being conducted upstairs and into a bedroom at the front of the house. The windows were tightly shut against the sun, and a strong and unmistakable smell of dog filled the room. He looked with sudden inquiry in the direction of the bed, remembering the picture of the wolf sitting up in cap and night-gown in the bed of Red Riding Hood's grandmother. But it was undoubtedly a real old lady who lay there, though she had big ears and big eyes and big teeth like her daughter. Her hair was snow-white, in discord with her sharp, ill-tempered features.

Julia shut the door behind him and he heard her go downstairs. He crossed the room with a conventional word of apology for intruding on her. As he reached the bed with outstretched hand, a small, pointed, damp-looking, hairy, toothless head came out from under the bedclothes. Even while he gazed at it with disgust he was relieved that there was a real, natural explanation for the smell of dog. This had once been a dog, a very small Yorkshire terrier. He could not say whether it was age or sheer wear and tear that had reduced it to its present state. Mrs. Hearn did not shake hands. Instead, she lifted out the wretched animal and put it into his hand. It required a tremendous moral effort not to drop it with a squelch on the floor. It was like being handed a live rat.

"Just put My Friend down, if you please," said Mrs. Hearn, and added querulously: "I think he has picked up fleas."

Henley did as he was told, with careful precision. He found himself unable to shake hands with the old lady now and determined to assume that the business with the dog was a substitute. She said crossly:

"Sit down, young man. Why should I strain my neck to look up at you. Take a chair and sit down."

He lifted forward a straight chair and sat at the foot of the bed, while she watched him eagerly. Then she said:

171

"I remember you. You used to be at the hotel. I didn't know you were in the police. Have you come about Mr. Reid?"

Now he realized that she was delighted to see him. She had always been an inveterate gossip, he knew, and no doubt she welcomed every visitor who came her way.

"Tell me what happened to Mr. Reid," she said, and added querulously: "Julia never tells me anything. I think she takes pleasure in keeping things from me."

"Of course you know that Mr. Reid was poisoned," he began.

She gave a little shriek of delight.

"Poisoned! How dreadful! I wouldn't have wished it for the world."

But she chuckled with the purest pleasure. A series of little answering squeaks came from under the bed, where My Friend had come to rest, and was apparently listening eagerly. Pat moved his chair a little way from the bed as he went on:

"Yes, it is dreadful. And, of course, I must find out how it happened. We don't know very much about Mr. Reid, and I thought that you might be able to help us since he was your landlord until you came here."

"Yes. He never did anything for us except collect the rent. It was a great satisfaction to be able to leave that house and come to live here. My Friend bit him in the ankle the day before we moved."

This time the answer came from under the dressing-table. Pat strangled a wild giggle and remarked solemnly:

" 'Well said, old mole! canst work i' the earth so fast?' "

Then he had to spend five minutes assuring Mrs. Hearn that he had not insulted her. It was only because she could not bear to cut short such a promising conversation that she forebore from turning him out of the room. Presently he was saying:

"This was a very fortunate chance for you. It's not easy to get a good house in Dangan. How long had you lived in the other house?"

"Almost seven years. My daughter was a singer, you know."
Henley nodded. "She was at the height of her powers when I
first became ill, and she gave up everything without a moment's
hesitation to come and look after her poor old mother."

She made it sound like Covent Garden, at the very least.
Henley knew that Julia had been about to sing at a series of
concerts in which it would not have mattered if she had failed,
but in which spectacular success would almost certainly have
assured her of further contracts. She certainly was the build of
a singer. He knew that Nature would not normally allow all
that good meat to go to waste.

"But then Reid was only your landlord for part of the time?"

"Yes. Before that the house belonged to a Mr. Ryan who
lived in Dublin. When he sold Fairy Lawn to Mr. Reid, our
house and a few others went with it. I must say that Mr. Ryan
was just as bad as Mr. Reid. He never came near the place at
all."

"Then you were not friendly with Mr. Reid," said Pat, in
what he hoped was a disappointed tone.

"Neither was I friendly with the plumber," she said coldly.

It was no wonder to Pat that Reid had done his best to let
the house fall down around her. He had certainly had a satisfactory revenge, with a leaky roof and inadequate drainage
with which to annoy her.

"I'm sure you'll find your new landlord much better," he said.

"I have not met him yet," she said, "but I have heard that he
is quite charming. I have been hoping every day that he will
call on me."

"And Miss de Cogan is very friendly with Miss Hearn," he
went on. "You are certainly very fortunate."

But Germaine was another story, it appeared.

"She's fully twenty years older than Julia," the old lady said.
"I don't consider her good company at all for the child. When
a girl begins to go about with older women it lessens her chance
of making other friends."

173

Henley wondered academically if there were a man in the length and breadth of Ireland who would take on Julia as a wife even if she had been fifteen years younger. Perhaps a very small man would have liked her, one who felt in need of protection, or of a windbreak on a cold day. Whatever the reason, it was clear that Mrs. Hearn did not like Germaine. They certainly would have no common interests or sympathies, and neither would have been likely to compromise.

"When I was in Dangan, on a former occasion, Miss de Cogan was living with her brother," he said innocently.

"Yes, it was well for us that they fell out," said Mrs. Hearn complacently. "This house was almost rebuilt when she came to live here. That's why it is so comfortable now."

"I wonder why they quarrelled?" he said thoughtfully.

But she did not know why. She would have given anything to have been able to tell him, but Germaine had been careful, and no hint of the reason had reached the old lady.

"I asked her about it," she said regretfully, "but she would tell me nothing. I don't like people who make too many secrets. She just said that they had decided not to live together any more, and that there were no ill feelings on either side. Well, of course, I didn't believe *that*. I think she trusted Sir Miles not to give her away because he was such a gentleman. But I think that if we heard the whole story, Germaine would not come so well out of it."

"But surely a lady of her years could have no disgraceful secrets," he said in a shocked tone.

She took up the suggestion at once with horrible eagerness, so that he felt he might as well have cast doubts on Germaine's morals in so many words.

"The very thing I thought myself," she said, "though it's not a very nice thought. With all those men around the place, I'm sure Sir Miles felt she would be better out of the way. Not that she wouldn't have had more opportunities living here alone," she finished reflectively.

174

She was a nasty old thing, and no mistake, thought Pat as he stood up to go. She had not helped him much, for her suggestion about the reason for Germaine's leaving Dangan House was absurd. Evidently the old lady's mind ran on these lines habitually, but Henley thought that Germaine's did not. Still he felt that this rather unsatisfactory conversation had served to strengthen his original opinion that the reason for the quarrel had been somehow discreditable to Germaine. Mrs. Hearn, with her long probing nose, had scented this and had leaped with delight to an obvious conclusion. There was no escape now from questioning Germaine herself.

If Germaine had wished to poison Reid she would have done so, Pat felt, with the same impersonal thoroughness with which she would put down an old dog.

Absent-mindedly, he shook hands with Mrs. Hearn and went out of the room, hardly hearing her request that he hand her back her wretched little dog.

Outside in the garden Julia was still weeding.

"Well," she said, "how was Mother on ancient history?"

"Very helpful, thank you," said Pat politely, and left her staring after him.

18

As he walked along the quiet road back to the village, Pat found himself savouring the peaceful afternoon stillness. It was not yet twenty-four hours since he had first heard of Reid's death. The recollection of the people he had interviewed since then almost made his head spin. Because they all lived so close together it had been too easy to rush from one to the other at breakneck speed, leaving no time for reflection in between. There had been no useful delays in which he would have had to sit down and quietly think out the implications of each person's statement. He would have dearly loved to spend the whole afternoon fishing, but he feared that the authorities would not have accepted this as a sign that he was proceeding enthusiastically with the business of apprehending Reid's murderer.

The indefatigable Lawlor had done the spadework of finding out how each of their suspects had spent the afternoon of Reid's death—or rather he had found out as much as they wanted to tell him. But Pat had not had time to sift this information and examine it closely, though he knew of at least one loophole that it contained.

Almost opposite Reid's gate, when he reached it, he saw an old stone stile leading up into the high field above. He could see long grass waving up there, and the temptation was too much for him. With a quick glance up and down the road, to see that no one was in sight, he ran up the steps of the stile and threw himself down on the soft warm grass. His old tweed suit would be covered with bits of dried grass and leaves, but that would do it nothing but good, he thought contentedly.

A narrow footpath, only barely discernible, wriggled its way from the stile across the field. This was the way that Reid must have gone yesterday to Dangan House, whose roofs, Pat knew, were just out of sight behind the hill. There was no other satisfactory explanation for the fact that no one had seen Reid on the afternoon of his death. Georgie Fahy had not missed him when he had gone out, so that he must have gone on foot. True to his type, Reid had never walked if he could drive. If he had gone by road to Miles's house, he would certainly have taken out his car to do so. And if he had planned to go across country, he would normally have called on Georgie to saddle his horse. But the horse had remained in the stable and the car in the garage, and Reid had arrived at Dangan House unnoticed. Henley felt that if he could discover the reason of Reid's unusual behaviour, he would be well on the way to knowing the motive for his murder.

It was particularly aggravating that no one had seen him, because there was not the smallest indication of the time of his arrival. When James had found him he had been dead only a few minutes, according to Dr. Donovan. This, taken with the knowledge of the length of time it took for the poison to kill him, should have discovered the place in which he had drunk the poison. A simple subtraction sum and a knowledge of Reid's movements were all that should have been necessary. But, unfortunately, the time in which nicotine could have killed him was variable.

Now there were two possibilities, equally plausible. Reid could have swallowed the poison at home, probably in the company of the murderer, and could then have hurried across the field to Dangan House. He could have been taken ill on the way, and have slipped into the house quietly, hoping to recover before he would have to meet anyone. The other possibility was that he had arrived at the house, and had been admitted by the murderer, who would since have denied all knowledge of him. He could have been led quietly into the library, given a drink of whisky and the poison, and chatted to pleasantly

177

until he passed away. Reid's habit of tossing off his glass of whisky in one gulp would have been a great convenience to his murderer, for he would have swallowed the poison before he could detect the taste.

If Reid had been killed at Dangan House, several things were known about the murderer. Firstly, he must have been familiar with Reid's drinking habits. This presented no complications, for anyone who knew Reid at all could have known that he drank whisky at every idle moment. Next, the murderer must have known his way around Dangan House. Most of Reid's acquaintances qualified there. The inhabitants of the house, including the servants, came first, of course, but after them would come Mrs. Hooper, Captain Merlin, Jane Merlin, Martin Doyle, even Julia Hearn. Any of these need only have said that they were sure Miles would like Reid to have a drink, and then have firmly placed a glass in his hand. Reid's reaction would have been automatic. If he had been poisoned at home, as Lawlor had pointed out, he would have poured the fatal drink himself. If his attention could have been diverted for a moment, the addition of the poison would have been easy. Stretched there on his back, with his hands behind his head, looking up at the clear blue sky, Henley began to reconstruct the little scene in his mind. A lone bird cruised across above him, and his mind went delightfully blank. A moment later he was on the brink of sleep. He rolled over, and after a moment stood up and began to brush off his clothes.

"Oh, wretched, wretched Reid," he thought moodily. "Why could he not have died a decent, natural death like an ordinary man?"

He stalked across the road in belligerent mood, and marched up the avenue to Reid's house.

He knew that Maggie had seen him coming, for he had spotted her at an upstairs window. But she kept him waiting for five minutes on the steps before she opened the door. When she did so at last she tried to look surprised.

"I thought we had finished with you," she said coldly.

"Perhaps," said Henley, "but I have not finished with you."

He pushed past her into the hall and opened the door of the drawing-room.

"In here, please!"

She did as she was told, and stood stiffly in the middle of the floor.

"Well?" she said with a practised glare, calculated to curl him up.

"What's this I hear from Sergeant Lawlor about your clearing away Mr. Reid's supper last night?" asked Henley menacingly.

She closed her eyes and said contemptuously:

"Sergeant Lawlor is a very ignorant man."

"Why did you do it? Didn't you know that we would want to see everything untouched? How can we——"

"Excuse me, Inspector Henley," said Maggie with powerful dignity. "I know nothing of these things. I am not accustomed to having my employers murdered. Next time, perhaps I'll be better able for the situation."

Seeing that she was more than able for him, he decided to change his method.

"Since the things were cleared away," he said, "perhaps you could tell me what was there."

But she could not. She had laid the table with knives and forks, plates, cup and saucer and one large glass, but she could not remember whether there had been more than one glass there when she had cleared away. It would have been fortunate if she had found two glasses, and if she had remembered it, but Pat knew that that sort of luck is rare. In any case, Reid and his murderer were more likely to have had their drink in the drawing-room. He made one or two threatening noises at Maggie, just for practice, and then went out to look for Georgie Fahy.

But here again he learned nothing new. Georgie was mowing

the grass on a delightful little sunken lawn at the side of the house. He seemed glad to be interrupted.

"I don't know is there any use in keeping up the place now that His Lordship is dead," he said. "No one has told us what to do. Will it be sold now, would you say?"

"I have no idea," said Henley. "You just carry on as usual until someone tells you to stop."

Georgie made a half-hearted effort to pump Pat, but he soon gave it up for lack of encouragement. He had not heard a car drive up to the door the day before, he said.

"Didn't I tell Sergeant Lawlor that? I was mowing the grass the same as I am now, and the old machine makes as much noise as a motor car."

It was a little petrol-driven machine, and it would certainly have masked the sound of a car engine. In any case, there was nothing to prevent the visitor from coming on foot. Georgie edged up to him.

"You couldn't by any chance take Maggie away and hang her?" he said hopefully. "There's no one would miss her."

"I'm afraid you haven't much respect for the law," said Pat.

"Down my part of the country we have our own law," said Georgie nonchalantly. "We don't encourage the Guards to be coming around asking questions and expecting right answers to them. Of course, here it's different, I know. They'd be killing each other here every day of the week if someone didn't put a stop to it. Living so near Dublin makes them uppish, I suppose."

He shook his head over metropolitan savagery. Pat left him then, regretting that he was too busy to stay and hear more. As he walked down the avenue he decided that there was nothing further to be learned at Reid's house. The spirit of Reid, which had seemed to be about the place in the morning, was now departed. On former occasions of a similar sort, Pat had had this fancy. It had been as if, for a short while after his death, the owner of his house had returned to collect some necessary luggage, perhaps, for his journey into the next world, and had

180

gone on his way at last, with a high, whining, gnat-like sound, leaving a clean blankness where he had been. Afterwards the house could wait coolly and impersonally for the next occupant to take possession.

Merlin's house, when he reached it, had an air of ugly unrest, although there was no one about. He rang the bell and waited for a minute. Then he heard a quick step in the hall and the door was opened by Merlin himself. He looked very cheerful and happy, and almost normal, and in that moment Pat realized with a little shock that Jane had inherited a large part of her good looks from her father. When he was younger, and before his inner meanness and greed had begun to show on his face, he must have been a handsome, attractive man. He held the door wide and said jerkily:

"Come in, Henley, come in. I'm all alone. Jane has gone over to de Cogan's place. Did you know she was very friendly with him? Yes, indeed. I'm hoping for great things there."

He led Pat into the front room in which they had talked in the morning.

"Sit down, Henley," he said solicitously, and herded him into a chair. "How are you getting on with the work?"

"Not too badly," said Pat carefully. "Have you thought of anything else that would help me?"

He held out his cigarette case to the Captain, who took one and pulled its head off with a sudden, savage movement.

"Doyle," he said. "You get after him. Don't mind anyone else."

Henley struck a match and gravely lit the remainder of the Captain's cigarette for him, and then lit his own. As he threw the spent match into the fireplace he said casually:

"Yes, I've been to see Doyle."

"Did he give himself away?" asked Merlin eagerly, hitching himself forward in his chair. "Did you find out how he did it?"

"I'm afraid I didn't get very far with him," said Pat, "but I'll be seeing him again." He watched Merlin carefully as he went on: "I don't think Reid disliked Doyle at all. He seemed to want to make friends with him."

"Did Doyle tell you that?"

Pat nodded.

"Doyle is a terrible liar," said Merlin. "It's easy for him to say that now, when Reid is dead. Reid hated Doyle, on account of Jane."

His eyes flickered around the room, and his hands began to twitch and shake so that he dropped his cigarette on the carpet. While he was scrabbling on the floor to pick it up, Henley got up and went across to the window. Standing there, looking out at the garden, he wondered what to do next. Merlin was in such a nervous state that it hardly seemed right to continue to question him or to encourage him to talk, but there was still one important thing that he wanted to do. Like an answer to prayer, he saw Lawlor at the garden gate, fumbling with the latch. With his presence to back him up, Pat felt justified in following the course he had planned. He tapped on the window-pane. Lawlor looked up and Pat beckoned to him to come into the house. He remembered that Merlin had left the door open. Then he turned back towards the Captain and said:

"I think Reid was beginning to change his mind about Miss Merlin."

"Nonsense," said Merlin querulously. "Fellow was crazy about her."

"Yes, I'm sure he had been very much attached to her," said Pat, "but I think something had happened to change that."

"Nothing had happened," said Merlin. "Only a few days ago he went into town specially to buy her an engagement ring."

"Did he give it to her?" asked Pat softly.

"He hadn't given it to her," said Merlin, "but I know he was going to. He told me the day he bought it. I didn't hurry him. I knew I need only wait and that I'd see Jane wearing it one day, and then everything would be settled."

He was looking sideways at Pat while he said this, his eyes screwed up and an expression of cunning on his face. Pat said:

"What do you know about his will?"

At that moment the door of the room opened and Sergeant Lawlor came silently in.

"His will?" said Merlin. "What about it?"

"I want you to tell me," said Pat. "We found a will in his house, drawn up in favour of your daughter. You knew about it, I think?"

"Of course," said Merlin blandly. "I told you I had to provide for my daughter."

"You have seen the will?"

"Reid brought it in one evening," said Merlin, and he could not forbear a happy little chuckle. "He had spent the evening writing it out, and he wanted to show it to me. He knew how I worried." He licked his lips. "It left everything to Jane, except the house. I told him he should have left her that too, but he laughed and said it was too expensive to keep up. So I said that was thoughtful of him——"

Suddenly he stood and looked at Lawlor.

"What are you doing here?" he asked sharply. "Why are you asking these questions, Henley? Jane will get the money, won't she? Won't she?"

Pat almost felt sorry for him, at that moment. He said slowly:

"Reid had not signed the will."

Merlin's mouth came slowly open, and he looked from one to the other of them incredulously. Pat turned away, already wishing that he had said nothing, and still wondering what the Captain would tell him as soon as he had recovered himself enough to speak. He heard Lawlor's voice in rough sympathy say:

"Ah, now, Captain Merlin, don't take it so hard."

Then there was a deadly little silence. Pat whirled around, just in time to see Merlin slide to the floor like a snake. Over his body, he stared into Lawlor's eyes.

19

The next half-hour was a nightmare. Between them, Lawlor and Pat lifted Merlin and got him on to the horrible Madame Récamier sofa that stood against one wall of the room. They put his head on the little hard sausage-shaped cushion and looked at him silently for a moment. Then Pat said:

"Stay with him, Lawlor. I'm going next door to telephone for Donovan."

With his head in a whirl, he hurried across to Reid's house, pushed his way past Maggie and grabbed at the telephone. At last he heard Donovan's voice at the other end of the wire. He said nothing but:

"Come to Merlin's at once, please," and hung up.

Maggie sniffed at his elbow. In two shakes he would have wept on her bony shoulder, if he had not been morally certain that she would have bitten him. He hesitated whether to summon Jane Merlin from de Cogan's house, and at last decided not to. He had no proof that she was there. Her father thought she had gone there, but it was quite possible that she had not done anything of the sort. The last time he had seen her, she had looked remarkably like a worm about to turn. At last he telephoned to Martin Doyle at the mill and asked him to come to Merlin's house too. Doyle was beginning a series of questions, but Pat hung up.

He was angry with himself for not having foreseen what the impact of his news on Merlin would be. The very fact that Merlin had been almost sane this afternoon had ensured that he had fully understood the meaning of what he was told, and the result had been the complete ruin of his little dream world.

Pat was experienced enough to know that Merlin's collapse could have very serious consequences. Even in a younger man such a sudden reaction would be alarming. And it was a difficult question whether he had collapsed because he had poisoned Reid and had failed to profit by it, or because Reid's death had been a shock and the second shock had been too much for him. Even if he had not poisoned Reid himself, he must have been hugging himself at his foresight in having got him to make his will in favour of Jane. With a few words, Pat had snatched his sackfuls of gold away.

While the layman in him was full of pity for Merlin, his other self, habitually dressed in policeman's uniform, was already rubbing its little hands and shaking its cunning head and waggling its long searching proboscis in anticipation of the effect of Merlin's collapse on the rest of its list of suspects, and on one hard-shelled suspect in particular.

He arrived at Merlin's door just as Donovan's car reached the gate. He waited while the doctor got out and slammed the door and came up the path almost at a run.

"What's going on here?" he demanded, as he reached the porch where Henley was waiting.

"Merlin," said Henley shortly.

He led him inside silently and left him with Lawlor. A few minutes later the Sergeant came out.

"The Captain has had a stroke," he said. "Dr. Donovan wants to get him into hospital. He says he's doubtful if he'll recover."

Avoiding Pat's eye, he went down the path to telephone for the nearest ambulance.

Before Lawlor came back, Doyle drove up to the gate in a cloud of dust. Pat had been watching out for him from the steps, for he had not wanted to go back into the room where Merlin was. As he walked slowly down the path, Doyle slammed the door of his car and came running in.

"Where's Jane? What's happened?" he demanded, gripping Henley by the shoulder.

"It's her father," said Pat, gently shaking off the clutching hand. "He's had a stroke."

"Oh!" Doyle paused. "I suppose it was coming to him. How bad is he?"

"Dr. Donovan is with him now. He's bad enough. The doctor is sending him to hospital, of course."

"But Jane can't stay here by herself."

Henley looked at him wearily, and wondered if he would some day behave like this, if he fell in love.

"Miss Merlin is not here now," he said. "I want to tell her what has happened. Do you know where she is?"

"No. I wasn't going to see her until this evening." Suddenly he was shouting. "You've been persecuting her. You told me so this morning. God knows where she is now——"

"There's no need to assume the worst," said Pat. "I left her in very good humour."

Doyle looked at him incredulously, but did not call him a liar. Pat went on:

"Would you take on the job of finding her and telling her the news? I'm going to Dangan House. You can get in touch with me there." As Doyle started down the path again he added: "She could spend the night at the hotel, if she doesn't want to come back here. I would have no objection to that."

Doyle started to ask rudely what Pat had to do with it, but he got no further than a word or two before he seemed to think better of it. He shut his mouth angrily and stamped off. Pat waited for Lawlor, who came back a few minutes later, and then he set off for Dangan House on foot, by way of the village.

As he passed the post office he glanced at the clock and saw with surprise that it was after five. The whole afternoon had slipped away unnoticed, between resting in the field and interviewing Reid's servants and frightening Merlin nearly to death. As he passed the hotel he glanced longingly at a short but con-

186

vincing notice outside the door which said: "Have a glass of Guinness when you're tired." The portrait of a creamy glass of stout was so lifelike that he could almost have licked it with his hot tongue. But duty called him on to plague the de Cogan household, and he walked firmly past. Doyle's car was parked at the hotel, he noticed. He had not been able to resist the advertisement, it seemed, or perhaps he was inside booking accommodation for his Jane.

At this point in his reflections he was no more than a yard or two beyond the hotel door. A little scuffle within the porch suddenly attracted his attention. He stepped back quickly and silently, and stood looking in. What he saw was fortunately not visible from the street, except perhaps to the people living directly opposite the hotel.

Doyle had found Jane, all right. One look at her was enough to tell Pat how she had spent the time since last he had seen her. She wore no coat over her crumpled cotton dress. Her hair was tousled and her beautiful, childlike blue eyes were glazed. Gin, Pat guessed, looking at her judicially, and reflecting on the strange power of heredity. Doyle was supporting her by the shoulders, and she seemed to have difficulty in holding her head up. Her eyelids drooped, and she wore the serene, happy expression of Rossetti's Beatrice. Doyle by contrast looked distressed and angry. He shook her a little and whispered:

"Stand up straight, Jane." She smiled sweetly and vacantly and he shook her again. "Do you want to make it impossible for us to live in Dangan?"

Suddenly he caught sight of Inspector Henley, who had stepped forward into the doorway. Martin Doyle's face grew suddenly red as he snarled:

"Snooping again, Henley?"

Pat raised his eyebrows.

"You need help, I think," he said mildly. "Miss Merlin has had a shock. Could you bring her to your house, if we got her to the car?"

187

Doyle made no apology for his rudeness, but he turned his face away as he mumbled:

"My housekeeper is away to-day. I wouldn't know what to do with her."

Pat suppressed an impatient sound.

"Would you bring her to Dangan House then? Miss de Cogan would look after her. Have you told her about her father yet?"

"No. How could I?"

"She'll need another woman to look after her," said Pat, and waited for Doyle to see the sense of this. "She could go to bed there and sleep for a while. She's been having a very bad time from her old man, and doing too much housework as well, probably. You can't blame her for this."

"I'm not blaming her."

Doyle put his arm around her protectively and glared belligerently at Pat, who said:

"All right, all right. Then we're all happy. Come along now and we'll get her into the car."

But before they could do so the inner door from the hall opened and Paul Walsh came out.

"I'm awfully sorry about this, Doyle," he said, his expression the picture of a distressed gentleman. "I had no idea it was going on, or I'd have stopped it. Joe shouldn't have served her. I came in and found him just handing her another drink. He seemed hardly to know what he was doing. She hadn't even paid for any of them——"

"I'll pay for them," said Doyle savagely. "You can go to hell."

"I don't want your money," said Walsh stiffly. "I only mentioned it because I wanted to explain that Joe is in no condition to be working."

"Then why did you let him work?" said Doyle excitedly. "You're not fit to own a hotel. You're too much of a little gentleman to work——"

"At least I don't poison my enemies," said Walsh with sudden force and marched back into the hall.

Pat heard him go into the office and slam the door. He looked curiously at Doyle, and then he put out his hand to support Jane, for Doyle would have dropped her. He had gone white, and he wore a look of frightening surprise, like a man who has seen the solid earth move apart before his very feet. Now Henley understood the significance of Walsh's remark when he had heard the news of Reid's death. He had said:

"How short-sighted of him. There was no need to do that."

Henley thought that he was suggesting that Reid had committed suicide, but it now seemed that he had been referring to Reid's obvious enemy, Doyle. For all his appearance of being made of bone from the neck up, it seemed that somewhere within Walsh there was a slowly ticking brain. For ordinary purposes this was not much use, but with its assistance he was able to draw attention to points that other people had missed, long after they had missed them. Henley was rather inclined to cross Walsh off his lists of suspects now, but he had not yet made up his mind about Doyle. His present expression of shocked surprise could be that of a man found out, as easily as it could betoken the reception of a new idea. He tapped Doyle on the shoulder and said:

"Come along, old man. We can't do any more good here."

Doyle shook himself awake and they half-carried Jane down the steps without further incident. Already Henley felt as if he had been standing in that porch all day. He prevailed on Doyle to sit in the back seat with Jane while he drove the car himself, and he noticed with irritation that the brakes were unreliable. It was typical of the disorganized state of Doyle's mind, he thought, that he would not keep his car in good order. It was astonishing that he was able to run his mill so efficiently while his private life was in such a state of chaos. Henley determined to inform Lawlor about the state of the brakes. Lawlor would come around the question in such a fatherly way that Doyle would have to have them repaired. Otherwise he would certainly kill a resident of the village and spend years in gaol for manslaughter, thought Henley gloomily.

Outside Dangan House he switched off the engine and turned to look at the passengers in the back seat. Jane had gone to sleep, and Doyle glared over her head, which was resting on his chest. Pat said briskly:

"Wait here for a moment while I explain what has happened."

He got out of the car without waiting for a reply, and went up the steps. James answered the bell, and led him into the drawing-room where Germaine was sitting alone, half-heartedly making up household accounts. He told her that he had Jane Merlin outside in Doyle's car.

"She's drunk as an owl, poor thing," he said, "and Martin Doyle is standing over her ready to bite anyone who comes along. Her nuisance of a father has just had a stroke, and someone will have to tell her when she recovers. I thought you might be good enough to give her a bed for the night——"

Germaine was already on her way outside. Henley shut the door carefully after her, and walked across to look out of the window at the side of the house. He was determined not to hear the little scuffling sounds of Jane being escorted upstairs, for the less he had to do with her the better for his own peace of mind. He deeply disliked being involved in the personal lives of other people, but, apart from his profession, in ordinary charity he could not entirely cut himself off from them. Already he had found that he could not solve Reid's murder without probing into the guarded secrets of innocent people. The way that Doyle and Walsh were behaving was typical of the effect of violence on shallow thinkers. One instinct always predominated—that of self-preservation, probably the least noble of man's instincts and certainly the ugliest to watch in operation. The fact that it always happened like this was no help. It never failed to set his nerves tingling, so that he was

190

sure he felt as guilty and as watchful as the murderer did. He almost envied Merlin, the ease with which he had had his stroke, the moment that life became too much for him.

Germaine did not come back, and Pat could not bring himself to send for her. The sun drowsed on the bright garden as if night would never fall, and he sat on the window-seat without moving, and watched the stillness. Doyle had not gone away, for he would have heard the engine of the car. A blackbird flew on to the window-sill and looked at him with a question in his little watchful round eye.

"Wasting my time, old boy," said Pat softly. "That's what I'm doing."

Through the open window he heard feet on the gravel, approaching slowly. The blackbird flew away. Pat slipped off the window-seat and stepped back into the room, out of sight. He was not ready for conversation yet. He wanted the news about Merlin to spread through the house before he would next appear. The footsteps came closer, and he moved to one side of the window so that he would be able to see who was there.

It was Miles, coming from his conversation with Barne, walking like an old man, with slow, heavy steps and bent head. He passed out of sight, and Henley came back thoughtfully to his seat at the window.

Something had happened to Miles, he was certain, and it was his business to find out at once what it was. Perhaps this was the moment also to ask him what he knew about the quarrel between Germaine and her brother, Sir Miles. It seemed possible that he would catch Miles off his guard now, and learn a number of things that he wanted to know. A fine way to repay hospitality, he thought grimly, as he started for the door.

The hall was deserted and the front door stood open. He found Martin Doyle's car still outside. He wondered where Germaine had put Doyle to wait for Jane to wake up. He did not want to meet him again, if he could avoid it.

There was no sign of Miles, and it was a moment before Pat realized that he must have gone around to the side of the house. He went after him, and presently saw him ahead, on his way to the back avenue. If he were going to the village, Pat decided that he would wait until later for his talk with him. He held back therefore until Miles reached the bridge, when he climbed slowly down the little bank on to the river's edge. Realizing that he was intending to go for a walk alone, Henley hurried forward to join him.

20

When Miles opened the door of the office, Barne looked up impatiently from the desk. When he saw who was there, however, he said apologetically:

"Come along in, Mr. de Cogan. I thought it was one of those wretched policemen."

Miles came across to sit on the only other chair, saying:

"I've hardly seen them at all to-day. They seem to be concentrating on Reid's household. I wish the whole thing were finished with." He accepted a cigarette from Barne. "What did you think of Inspector Henley?"

"A bit flippant, for my taste," said Barne. "But he's young, and it must be difficult to feel other people's troubles."

"I like him," said Miles. "I must say I was very pleased to find a friendly-disposed person among the Guards. It was unfortunate that poor Reid came here to die. How do you think it will affect me?"

"Not very much," said Barne judicially. "After all, you hardly knew him. You'll have to go to the inquest, of course, and so will James and myself, because we were the first to find him. But the coroner will be very nice to you, you'll find. You have nothing to worry about, really."

"Could you do the talking for me?" Miles asked hopefully, but Barne shook his head.

"I think it would be better not," he said. "You are the owner of the house, you see, and it's you they'll want to question. If you seem to be avoiding answering them, they'll wonder what you have to hide. Then, because I'm a solicitor, if I spoke for you, they might get the idea that I was doing so officially, if you understand me, and this again might make them suspicious. I take it, of course, that you have no—information about Reid's death?"

"None whatever," said Miles.

He felt comforted by Barne's clear and simple statement of his position, although it seemed that he would not be able to avoid the unpleasant ordeal of the inquest. Barne knew his business, undoubtedly. Miles now felt that the unwilling hospitality that he had given Reid would be recognized by the coroner for exactly what it was. Hitherto he had feared that he would be questioned and badgered and trapped into false statements, so that the prospect of the inquest had become a sort of nightmare.

"Poor Tom," said Barne sadly. "Who would have foreseen such an end for him?"

"We have all been so shocked that none of us has had time to think of the personal side of it," said Miles. "I'm afraid you must have thought us very callous."

"No, no," said Barne with a sigh. "I understand how it is. He was foolish to have stirred up all that fuss about the road-house. I'm sure he didn't care two pins whether he built it or not. If I had seen him I should certainly have advised him to drop the whole thing. But it's too late now to say that."

"Then you think someone in the village got too excited about the road-house, and killed him?" asked Miles eagerly.

"Of course," Barne shrugged. "There is usually a simple explanation of this sort of thing. The Guards will have whoever did it within a day or two."

"You don't think it could have been suicide?"

"My first conclusion was that it was suicide," said Barne, "but now I'm not so sure. There must be a very good reason for suicide, and if there had been a reason I should certainly have known about it." He sighed. "I am going to make myself believe that Tom was killed in a motor accident. Yes, that is the best way to forget the whole thing."

"You certainly are a comfort," said Miles. He hesitated for a moment and then went on: "I hope you won't be shocked at what I'm going to ask you. I know you have a great respect for law and order, and so have I. But, as I see it, this is no one's business but my own."

Barne looked at him quizzically, but he said nothing. Miles stumbled for a moment and then said:

"It's about what I wrote to you, you know. What Reid said to me on the night before he died." Barne nodded and Miles went on: "I couldn't understand what he was getting at. At first I thought he wanted to tell me something, and then I came to the conclusion that he was threatening me."

"Surely not!" said Barne incredulously.

"I was astonished too," said Miles, "because I couldn't think what he would have against me. But then it appeared that he thought I had been concerned in the agitation. That was ridiculous, of course. I had only met him once or twice. I could have had no possible purpose in persecuting him." He shrugged. "I didn't argue with him for more than a word or two. In any case, he went off and gave me no chance to defend myself. But just before he went he said something that made me wonder. I don't remember the exact words that he used, but he seemed to imply that I had no title to live here. You remember I told you that in my letter."

Barne nodded and said:

"That was nonsense, of course. You saw the documents yourself. Everything was in order. I hope you haven't been losing your night's sleep over that."

"Well, you see," said Miles apologetically, "I had to take some heed of it. For all I knew, Reid could have known of the existence of a later will, or thought he knew of it." Barne began to speak but Miles held up his hand. "Now wait one moment while I explain. As you know, it was a great change for the better for me to come here. But if this is not mine, I want no part of it. I could go back to Dublin to-morrow and return

195

quite happily to my old occupations—and probably get paid more, too, since I've learned how to value myself. I could think of my weeks here as a pleasant unexpected holiday—except for recent events, of course, which might only serve to make it easier for me to part with it all."

"Are you really serious?" asked Barne in astonishment.

"Why not? I don't say that I would be glad to go, but I have not yet become a part of the place. I don't want something that is not mine. I am quite determined about that."

"I see." Barne pursed up his little mouth and cogitated. "I'm afraid you've been having a bad time. I didn't realize that you felt so deeply about it. But you can take it from me that unless something extraordinary happened, there is no later will. Tom could not have been hinting at that, whatever he was suggesting."

"Why are you so certain?"

"Because I was with Sir Miles the day before he died, and he mentioned you. James McDonagh was there. He'll tell you the same. Sir Miles didn't die suddenly, you know. He had several days in which to arrange everything, and he knew he was going to die."

"You didn't tell me this before."

"Did I not? Well, it didn't come up, I suppose. At any rate, Sir Miles said he hoped I would find you soon and that you would like the place as much as he did."

What a tiresome little fellow Barne was not to have told him this before now, Miles thought. A great wave of relief swept over him, so that he was quite unable to speak for a moment. This little bit of information, together with his co-operative plan for the mill, made it possible for him to resolve never again to doubt his right and his usefulness to Dangan.

"That brings us back to where I began," he went on at last. "I was going to ask you—not to mention my conversation with Reid to the police. Does that sound too illegal to you?"

196

Barne thought for a moment and then he said:

"I don't see any need to mention it. After all, it has nothing to do with the case, and it might only start them looking to you for possible motives for wanting Reid out of the way."

"That is just what I fear," said Miles. "I'm sure I could convince them in time that I had nothing to do with his death, but I don't want to have to go through all that. In any case, they have Merlin to go on with. He certainly had a motive, if anyone had."

He told Barne about the extraordinary conversation he had had with Merlin that very day. Barne's eyes gleamed with amusement.

"A fine direct approach," he said. "Shouldn't you tell the Guards about it?"

"I have done so," said Miles. "I told Inspector Henley at once."

"That should keep him busy," said Barne comfortably, "that and the village agitation. Village people get turned in on themselves. They are really capable of almost anything."

"Perhaps when I have the mill going differently it will help to turn them outwards," said Miles. "Have you had any time to draft that agreement?"

Barne laid down the pencil with which he had been fidgeting and looked directly at Miles.

"I have not drafted an agreement, because I wanted to have a talk with you first. I have to tell you at the outset that I think your plan won't work."

"Oh, come!" said Miles cheerfully. "It has worked in other places. Why not here?"

"Because you could not trust the very people on whom you would have to depend."

"Why not? We needn't do it all at once. We can begin in a small way, and gradually build up the business until we have doubled its value. It will make the Dangan people proud of their village."

"It should," said Barne gently. "But a great deal depends on the personality of the people concerned."

"I have no doubts about them," said Miles. "They are all full of enthusiasm. Doyle is a bit cross and uneasy, but that will soon change when he is allowed to expand the business. And the other men—why, one could not wish for better. And the best of them all is my own land-steward, John Wall, who will act as a sort of liaison officer between me and the men, so that all grievances will be stopped before they have time to develop."

Barne was silent, looking down at the paper-littered desk. Miles said sharply:

"Well, what is it? You know something. Don't hesitate to tell me."

"John Wall has been cheating you since you came," said Barne quietly.

Miles sprang to his feet.

"Nonsense!" he cried. "I'll have him in this moment. I don't believe it."

"Do you think I like the job of telling you?" said Barne. "Please let me finish."

"I'm sorry," said Miles at once, and sat down shakily. He rubbed his forehead with the back of his hand. "It's just that I can't believe—no, I won't say that."

He looked up at Barne and felt to his shame tears prickling behind his eyes. A little voice within him said, over and over: "Fool, fool, fool!"

Aloud he said:

"Please go on."

Barne said in a pleading tone:

"For heaven's sake don't take it so hard. It's a thing that often happens. A man can be quite honest with the person who first employed him. It often happens in factories and shops and places like that. Call it the frailty of human nature."

He looked appealingly at Miles, who found this cliché absolutely devoid of consolation. Again Miles said:

198

"Go on, please."

Barne made a helpless little gesture with his hands.

"Wall may not have known that I would continue to do the farm accounts," he said. "I've spent most of the day on them, just as I happened to have the time, and to take my mind off other things. Sometimes a poor man like Wall thinks that a wealthy man would not miss a few pounds here and there." Miles nodded, knowing that this was true. "However, I'm so familiar with the estate and its affairs that it did not take me long to see what was missing."

Miles stood up and crossed to the desk.

"Show me," he said.

Barne spent ten minutes showing him, his tone of voice growing more and more apologetic as Miles became more coldly angry. At last Barne said for the eleventh time:

"And look here——"

"Yes, thank you. I see." Miles interrupted him with a sigh. "I have been an unconscionable fool." Barne twittered a little and Miles went on tiredly: "Yes, I should have known better than to trust my own judgment. How could I have thought that I was fit to start a whole new enterprise like this, or even to carry on after my cousin? I've been isolated too long——"

Suddenly he realized that he was talking aloud and that Barne was an eager, if a sympathetic, listener. There would be plenty of time for blaming himself later on, when he would be alone. Perhaps this was what Reid had been hinting at. Reid would never have been deceived by an employee; in fact, he had probably reviewed Miles's employees automatically and had guessed which one of them was cheating him. In a moment of despair, Miles wished that he had a mind like Reid, who had been wiser in his generation than Miles could ever hope to be. He put this thought away, however, recognizing it as unprofitable and self-indulgent. There were other and more useful things to be thought of, and a solution found for the present difficulty. He wished his head would clear, so that he could see

199

what was next to be done. Just now he saw Barne through a fog, and hated him unreasonably as the one who had disillusioned him.

Barne seemed to sense this, for he looked somewhat bewildered.

"There is no need to do anything in a hurry," he said. "Wall has no idea that we know what he has been at. You could think over my solution, and tell me later on if you would approve of it. I'll do the rest. You'll have no more trouble, I can promise you."

"What is your solution?" asked Miles, who saw none.

"To dismiss John Wall, of course," said Barne. "But I should give him a pension. He's an old man, and he has worked here all his life. It would not be right to be hard on him. He won't ask why he is being dismissed, because he'll guess that you have found him out. Then, if you never tell anyone the full story it will all die with Wall. He won't live long, by the way," Barne finished. "He's an old man, and this will be a shock to him."

Miles made no answer for a moment. Again he felt the tears behind his eyelids, but this time they seemed to trickle in a little acid stream from his very heart. How cool Barne was about it all! The legal mind felt no human emotions, apparently. As soon as he could trust himself to speak, Miles said huskily:

"And what about my co-operative scheme for the mill? What about Martin Doyle and the plan for expansion? What do you advise there?"

"I should drop it, if I were you," said Barne. "At least for the present."

"But the men know all about it," said Miles. "And Doyle will be terribly disappointed if we don't go ahead with it."

"Well, supposing you let Doyle make his pig-food," said Barne patiently. "That will keep him happy for the present. You can tell him there were difficulties about the other plans and that you would like more time to think them over. The

200

men of the village will accept the same excuse. They are accustomed to the gentry being capricious."

"I suppose that is the best we can do," said Miles dully. "I don't feel able to think it all out yet. Could we discuss it again later on?"

"Of course," said Barne. "May I give you a piece of advice. I hope you won't think it an impertinence?"

"I will not," said Miles with a bitter smile. "There must be very few people in Ireland from whom I couldn't learn something."

Barne was not offended at this ambiguous statement.

"It is simply this," he said slowly. "You would do very well not to take your new position here so seriously. It's not for nothing that the landed gentry isolate themselves from the people. Keep out of the village's way more. You've seen the ugly way they behave when someone crosses them. Make a routine for yourself—a little shooting or hunting or fishing. These are the traditional occupations of a country gentleman, and you could have a very pleasant life here if you found your company among the other people of your own kind. It's only a suggestion, of course," he finished hurriedly as he saw Miles's expression change. "But I'm afraid life will become difficult for you in Dangan if you don't conform to the traditions, that's all."

Miles thanked him gravely, and felt his spirit return a little. Life could not be entirely black as long as there were unconscious comedians like Barne to entertain him. He could even promise himself a laugh with Germaine over the solemnly given advice. As he left the office he decided to spend a long afternoon alone, in the course of which he would have to work out how best to disentangle himself and his village from the difficulties in which he had placed them.

In the hall he hesitated whether to go out into the inviting sunshine or to go up to his room. At last he went upstairs, because he could not face the possibility of meeting acquaintances and having to chat with them. In his present condition they would think that he had gone mad.

He brought a chair to his bedroom window and sat there for a long time, looking out over the quiet garden to the sunny fields. It was like Paradise, he thought, or a picture postcard in which every human being is wisely left out of the camera's vision.

Presently he heard the sounds of Jane being escorted upstairs, and Germaine's voice soothing Doyle. He had not the faintest idea what was happening, but in any case it seemed that Germaine was in charge. He waited until the sounds died away along the corridor and then he slipped out of his room and down the stairs. He saw Doyle's car at the front door, so he went into the dining-room and out by the french windows to the garden. The sudden blaze of light and colour struck him like an intolerable pain, so that his feet dragged on the gravel. He started for the front of the house, so confused that he had already forgotten why he had avoided the front door. With his head bent, he did not see Pat at the drawing-room window watch him go by.

21

When Miles and Inspector Henley returned from their walk it was almost dinner-time. They were both preoccupied, and they separated with no more than a word to go to their rooms. As Miles brushed his hair at the dressing-table he caught his own eye in the glass and paused, with the brush held aloft, to stare at the astonished face that looked back at him. In all his years in Dublin he doubted if he had had as many surprises as in the last few weeks. They had done him nothing but good. He felt stimulated and invigorated by them and he looked back on the years in which he had enjoyed a quiet life as a marvellously liberated snake might look back at his sloughed skin already beginning to dry in the undergrowth, while he slipped away to new freedom.

Henley was a delight to converse with. He was a man who met ugly reality in his daily work, but who had placed it properly in his scheme of things and would not allow it to leave its appointed pigeon-hole. Already he had helped Miles to stop being shocked at the wickedness of man, and to look further and find the writhing, tormented soul beneath.

This afternoon Miles had been on the edge of despair. Henley had hauled him back with a practised hand, and had asked to be rewarded with Miles's confidence. It would have been churlish to have refused. He grinned wryly at his reflection as he remembered the ensuing conversation.

When he reached the dining-room Germaine was already there. Barne appeared a moment or two later, and then Henley, apologizing for his lateness. But before they could sit down James announced Dr. Donovan, who said cheerfully:

"I had to come and find out how you were all getting on. I heard that Jane Merlin is here."

"Is she?" Miles raised his eyebrows and looked at Germaine, who nodded. "I didn't know. I've been out for a walk."

"I'll have a look at her later on," said Donovan looking meaningly at the table.

"Won't you have dinner with us first?" said Miles elaborately.

"That's an idea," said Donovan, delighted. "As a matter of fact, I haven't yet dined."

James was already laying another place, and a moment later they all sat down. Miles said:

"I saw Martin Doyle's car at the door. Has something been happening?"

"Captain Merlin has had a stroke," said Germaine. "Inspector Henley and Martin brought Jane here and I persuaded her to go to bed."

Very delicately put, thought Henley, who knew that Jane was still in a drunken sleep and was quite unaware of the state of her father's health. Barne was twittering and fluttering so that a corner of his napkin got into his soup. Germaine went on:

"It's very hard to be sorry this has happened. Jane would be far better off away from her father. She was such a bright, happy little thing when she first came home from school."

Donovan shook his head ponderously and said:

"I'm afraid the bold Captain is about to kick the bucket."

Henley put down his spoon and said gently:

"Perhaps it would be just as well."

There was a little silence for a moment, in which they could hear James breathing heavily over the vegetables. Miles found his appetite suddenly gone.

"Do you think Captain Merlin poisoned Mr. Reid?" Germaine asked in a flat voice.

"There are a few things still to be tidied up," said Henley. "We have to be quite certain of our ground, you see."

"Did he have the stroke when you charged him?" Donovan asked eagerly. "That often happens. I've seen it several times——"

"People accused of murder having strokes?" asked Miles incredulously.

"No, no," said Donovan. "I express myself badly. I have often seen people who have had a violent physical reaction, such as a stroke or a perforated stomach, after prolonged nervous tension."

"I haven't heard what poison was used," said Germaine, who had gone on with her soup in a determined way.

"Nicotine," said Pat. "Stuff you spray roses with. It kills the greenfly."

"We have gallons of it in a shed in the garden," said Miles quickly.

"I know," said Pat. "Merlin had not so much at his place, but he had enough. It takes very little to kill a man." He filled his spoon with soup and drank it in the midst of a tense silence before he went on: "A teaspoonful or even less would do it. The symptoms would be nausea and salivation, headache, dizziness, mental confusion, disturbed hearing and vision, faintness and prostration."

"Full marks," said Donovan dryly. "I know the book you got that out of."

"I got it out of the official report," said Pat. "Reid would have had convulsions, too, and difficulty in breathing. That would go some way towards explaining his appearance."

"Must we have this during dinner?" said Germaine mildly.

"Sorry," Pat mumbled. "Thought you'd be interested."

"I must say I think this is no place for such a discourse," said Barne, who had a high flush and was looking decidedly upset.

"Then we'll have no more of it," said Miles soothingly. "We'll talk about the state of the crops, and what's wrong with the country for a while."

But Barne still looked offended, and refused to be joked out

205

of his resentment. They finished dinner quickly and uneasily, and Miles was amused to see the disappointment of James when the subject of conversation became duller. Presently they stood up and looked at each other. Germaine moved towards the door.

"We'll have coffee in the drawing-room," she said.

"Could I have a word with you first?" asked Henley, while the others unconsciously crowded nearer.

She flashed a quick look at Miles, but he was looking at Pat's face.

"Of course," she said, with a nervous little laugh.

She seemed about to say more, but thought better of it and went out of the room, followed by Pat. A moment later the others came out into the hall and saw the library door close gently after them.

"To the drawing-room," said Miles purposefully, and led the remainder of his party there.

There was only Donovan and Barne, and he despaired of making conversation. Donovan's chat would be almost certain to give offence to Barne, who was being difficult this evening, though he had reason to be so. Miles sent Jenny away and busied himself among the coffee-cups, which took up several minutes. Donovan had fallen silent, a rare state with him, and Miles was about to announce some idiotic opinion on the weather when the door opened. James appeared, leading Julia Hearn.

Miles welcomed her so heartily that she raised her huge eyebrows at him. He planted her in a chair and brought her a cup of coffee. He could see her looking about for Germaine, but she did not ask for her. Instead she said:

"I had your Inspector Henley in this afternoon, interviewing Mother."

"What on earth for?" asked Miles. "He surely doesn't think she could know anything about Reid."

"He said she would be well informed on the local history,"

said Julia, "which is a very civil way of saying that she would know the gossip. And you must remember that Mr. Reid was our landlord."

No one made any answer to this.

"Captain Merlin has had a stroke," said Miles. "It seems the whole thing has been too much for him."

"Couldn't it mean that he poisoned Mr. Reid?" said Julia eagerly. "It's just the sort of thing he would think of."

"Henley hinted at that just now," said Donovan. "I said that I thought Merlin had a poor chance of recovery, and Henley said that it might be just as well if he died."

"That sounds rather like it," said Julia. "The only thing is that Jane was going to marry Reid. Surely Merlin would have done far better to let well alone."

Barne cleared his throat, looking worried.

"Well, as a matter of fact, that had all changed," he said. "I hardly know what to do, now that Merlin is in danger of death. You really think he won't recover, Donovan?"

"I should be very much surprised if he did," said the doctor.

"If you have any information you must give it to the police at once," said Miles earnestly.

"Must I?" said Barne waspishly.

"Well, certainly, if it has a direct bearing in the case," said Miles, rather disconcerted. "It seems you needn't fear that you will injure Merlin, because he's going to die anyway."

"Tell us what you know," said Julia in her deep voice, sounding unaccountably amused, "and we'll advise you whether to tell the police or not."

But Barne had to twitter for a few minutes, and wring his little hands before he would go on. It was Donovan who prodded him to the point by saying:

"After all, Barne, old boy, you're half a policeman yourself, just like me. Didn't you take an oath to defend the right and help to catch all the criminals, so that there would be more work for the lawyers?"

"That's just what is worrying me," said Barne. "I know I should tell, but I don't want to do an injustice to Tom Reid's memory."

There was a little silence. No one seemed willing to explain that Reid's memory was already so smirched that another little daub would make no difference. Then Miles said:

"Wouldn't it be worse if the police came to the conclusion that Reid committed suicide? Nothing could be more discreditable than that."

"If Merlin lives," said Barne at last, "he will certainly give himself away sooner or later. He's not really sane at the best of times, poor fellow."

"It seems certain that the Guards are on his track already," said Donovan. "When I said something about Merlin having a stroke when he was charged with the murder, Henley didn't deny it."

At that moment Germaine came into the room. She looked pale and upset, and there was a distinctly frightened look behind her eyes. Donovan and Barne turned eagerly towards her, as if they were about to shower questions on her. But Miles forestalled them smoothly by placing her in a chair between himself and Julia, and handing her coffee, while he glared over her head at Donovan. Then he said:

"Is Inspector Henley still in the library?"

"Yes," said Germaine. "He has settled down there with bundles of notes. He wants us all to stay here and wait for him."

"Mr. Barne has something important to tell him," said Miles. "I'm sure he wouldn't mind being interrupted for that." Barne hesitated, and Miles went on: "Come along. I'll go with you, if you're nervous. Where is Martin Doyle?" he asked suddenly.

"Upstairs with Jane," said Germaine. "I sent him up a tray, because he wouldn't come down to dinner. Doing the Fido-on-his-master's-grave business." She smiled wearily. "That's very catty of me."

"I'll tell James to send him in here if he comes down," said Miles standing up.

Barne got up reluctantly and followed him out of the room. In the hall they found Carr, in full uniform, standing squarely with his back to the door. The baize door to the kitchen closed with a swish, so that he knew Alice had been admiring her beloved in his glory. Carr stepped aside and said:

"You're supposed to stay in the drawing-room, gentlemen. That's the Inspector's orders."

He looked put out when Miles explained that they were going to find the Inspector. He glanced from the drawing-room door to the study door, obviously measuring the start that an escaping criminal would have on him if he left his post for a moment. He looked up to Heaven for guidance, and apparently got it, for a moment later he said:

"All right so. I'll come to the study door with you."

He marched across the hall in front of them and opened the study door, and then stood aside to allow them to pass into the room.

The menacing air of their escort and the grim appearance of Inspector Henley behind the desk struck Miles dumb for the first moment. Sergeant Lawlor was sitting at a table by the window laboriously writing on a sheet of foolscap. Miles edged along the wall like a schoolboy, with Barne at his elbow, until Pat said:

"Come along and sit down. Have you something to say to me?"

"Mr. Barne has decided to give you some information," said Miles.

He looked at Barne, who was now the less nervous of the two. His earnest expression was that of a man about to perform an unpleasant duty. He sat in the chair that Henley offered him, clutching his hands between his knees and frowning slightly. Henley said:

"What is it, Mr. Barne?"

Sergeant Lawlor had stopped writing and was listening intently.

"I hardly know whether I'm doing right," said Barne. "Everyone tells me that I should tell you what I know and now that Merlin is dying I don't see that it can do him any harm."

"Go on," said Henley softly.

"It's about the reason why Captain Merlin might have wanted to poison Tom Reid," said Barne apologetically. "You know that Tom was going to marry Jane Merlin and that Merlin was awfully pleased about it, on account of Reid's being so wealthy."

"Yes, I know about that," said Henley.

"Well, perhaps you didn't know that Reid was beginning to change his mind. He was getting tired of Jane, because she never had anything to say to him. He told me he was half inclined to look for a girl of his own kind and more his own age, who would be glad to marry him instead of being forced into it by her father. Oh, he was not deceived at all! about that part of the business. His pride was hurt, you see, and that meant a lot to him."

"This is very interesting," said Henley. "And where did the mill come in?"

"He had made a will in favour of Jane," said Barne impatiently, "and I suppose Captain Merlin killed him so that he would not have time to alter it. He left me his house in Dangan in that will, but I'm not sure that I want it."

"I said where did the *mill* come in?" said Henley.

"The mill? The mill had nothing to do with it."

"Oh, yes," said Henley. "The mill was the most important part of it."

"I'm afraid I know nothing about that," said Barne, standing up. "I don't know whether this has been of any use to you, but I was afraid you might have overlooked it."

"We had not," said Pat, "but it was thoughtful of you to tell us, in any case. Now if you can tell me what there was between

210

Reid and Martin Doyle, and what was Reid's interest in the mill——"

"I know nothing about that," said Barne again. "So far as I know, Reid had no interest in the mill."

"Oh, but he had," said Pat earnestly. "He wrote to Doyle about it. A very strange letter. And Mr. de Cogan has been telling me that he thinks the mill is very important. Isn't that so, Mr. de Cogan?"

Miles nodded and stammered his rehearsed piece.

"I always thought the mill was a gold-mine," he said. "I could never understand why you wanted me to get rid of it, Barne. It was only to-day that I realized that you wanted it for yourself."

Barne laughed without humour.

"I couldn't buy a mill," he said shortly.

"But Tom Reid could," said Pat, "and he wasn't going to let you off helping him."

Barne said, very softly:

"What nonsense, Mr. Henley. What utter nonsense." He moved towards the door.

"Mr. de Cogan has been telling me that you found John Wall cheating him," said Pat. "Strange how history repeats itself."

Barne turned around, looking sharply from one to the other, like a bird listening for the tunnelling of worms. Then, in a high, unreal tone, he said:

"Mr. de Cogan again! Why don't you ask him about his connection with Reid? Did you know he's holding back information? Did you know that? Ask him what Reid said to him on the night before he died. Ask him why he was damn glad to have Reid out of the way. Ask him what Reid said when he met him on horseback on the avenue."

"How did you know Reid was on horseback?" Miles asked gently.

22

"If Barne had kept his mouth shut", said Henley some hours later, "we would have had a hard job to catch him out."

He and Miles and Germaine were sitting in the drawing-room. Barne had been dispatched to Dublin in a plain van, attended by a number of large Guards, whose soft hearts were touched by the miserable, shrinking appearance of their prisoner. Miles had lit the fire, for Germaine had complained of the cold, although it was a mild evening. The orange blaze of the burning logs lit up the room. He had not switched on the lights, and the dimness was pleasantly restful.

Julia Hearn had gone home, having promised to visit Germaine in the morning. Dr. Donovan had been less delicate. Henley had almost had to push him, protesting, out of the front door. Donovan had been waiting for details of the story with such a lack of inhibition that Miles had found himself influenced to take a less personal interest in Barne's fate. He could not hope to be quite as detached as the doctor, and indeed he did not wish to be, but still he realized that it was no use sentimentalizing over what had happened. Only for his own part in trapping Barne, small though it had been, he knew that he would not have felt so uncomfortably guilty.

Martin Doyle was still upstairs with Jane, but Germaine had visited them and reported that Jane was awake and feeling much better.

"How did you light on Barne?" Miles asked from the depths of his armchair. "I thought him such a dull little man."

"Murderers are seldom clever," said Pat. "I found myself taking an interest in Barne quite early. I noticed that he never

212

lost his appetite, though his dearest friend had been poisoned. Whenever I remember this case I think I'll always hear the sound of Barne eating. Presently I became convinced that the quarrel between Miss de Cogan and her brother was the critical point of the case." He looked across at Germaine apologetically. "I was sorry to have to ask you about that."

"I'm very glad that you did," said Germaine. "I had never told anyone about it, and of course I was quite green inside from nursing my grievance. It was foolish of me not to have suspected Barne of having engineered the whole affair."

"May I know the story of the quarrel, Germaine?" said Miles.

"Of course, I should have told you long ago. It was the same idea as Barne tried to use between you and John Wall. Barne told my brother that I was stealing small sums of money by falsifying the household accounts." She shrugged. "I don't know what became of my sense of humour. Miles came along to me solemnly and told me that he had discovered my peculations, and so on. He wouldn't tell me who had told him. I was so angry with him for having listened to such a story that I decided there and then to leave the house. I did not realize that my brother was at the beginning of his last illness, or I should certainly have been more patient."

"As soon as I heard this," Henley went on, "I saw the hand of Barne. He made a bad mistake in trying to repeat his effect. Miss de Cogan had been so reticent about the reason of her falling out with Sir Miles that he thought she would never reveal it."

"But why did he want me to sack John Wall?" asked Miles.

"What he wanted was to sap your self-confidence, and put a stop to your plans for the mill," said Pat. "Barne was badly in debt. He felt that he couldn't afford to have you looking after your own affairs, because his opportunities for picking up easy money here and there would soon be reduced to nothing. He has just told us all about that part of it. He has been backing losers on the Stock Exchange for a number of years. And, most important of all, he wanted to be allowed to handle the large sum of money that Sir Miles had left lying in the bank."

"Forty thousand pounds," said Miles thoughtfully. "I would never have left that completely in his hands. Why, I hadn't even asked him to go on keeping the farm accounts for me. I was quite annoyed with him when I found that he had taken it on himself and doubly so when he told me of his so-called discovery. I think that even if John Wall had really been cheating me, I should have got rid of Barne."

"He was a bad psychologist," said Pat. "Sir Miles was not grateful to him either. He tells me that he was deeply disappointed that Sir Miles left him nothing in his will."

"My brother always thought of Mr. Barne as a sort of superior domestic animal," said Germaine.

"Where did Reid come in?" Miles asked.

"Barne had been cheating Sir Miles for years," said Pat. "When he died and Barne found that you had been living in poverty, he thought it would be very easy to carry on with his old game and start a very profitable new one. Reid had helped him on several occasions to keep dividends and rebates of income tax for himself, and Reid therefore felt that he had a hold over Barne. It was Barne's idea that you should be persuaded to sell the mill to Reid, who would soon develop it into the gold-mine that it should be. Barne would have a share of the profits, in return for his help, and he would be financially secure for the first time in his life.

"But very soon Barne found that you were not going to be as easily influenced as Sir Miles had been. You had lived this sort of leisurely life in your youth, and you slipped into it again without much difficulty. Barne had made the mistake of thinking that you would be overawed by Dangan, and that you would be afraid to do anything without consulting him. But within a few days you had Mrs. Hooper out of the house and Miss de Cogan back where she belonged. Barne got a real fright when he heard of this, and he decided that the only way to save his skin was for him to become an honest man—temporarily, at least.

"But Reid wouldn't let him. Reid had a real power complex. Barne was only in the business for the money. Reid was furious when Mrs. Hooper was sacked. It was on his suggestion that Barne had got Sir Miles to employ her. Reid had told Mrs. Hooper that he had influence with Sir Miles, because he knew that she would tell the natives of his home village what fine friends he had. This part of it is pathetically silly. He had been boasting to Mrs. Hooper that Miles would have to do what Reid told him. And he was furious also that the Hearns were no longer in his power. He had taken real pleasure in keeping them in discomfort in that nasty little house of his. Mrs. Hearn had slighted him on every possible occasion. She made no secret of that.

"He got after Barne and told him that he must get Miles to put Miss de Cogan back in the lodge and reinstate Mrs. Hooper. But Barne knew better than to try that. He dug his toes in. He tried to make Reid understand that they had underestimated Miles, but Reid would not see reason. He had promised Mrs. Hooper that he would have her back in Dangan House without delay. He had also set his heart on owning the mill. He decided that he would get into direct communication with Martin Doyle first and then force Barne to help him, with the threat of exposing Barne's dishonesty to Miles. Barne now saw no alternative to killing Reid."

"If he had told me all this I wouldn't have got him into trouble," Miles murmured.

"He couldn't risk it, he says," said Pat. "We always find these people the same. They can't risk exposure, but they can risk being indicted for murder. Their logic misses fire somewhere. Besides, there was the affair of Martin Doyle and the mill.

"Barne feared that if his honesty came into question at
215

all, the whole plot about the mill would come out. He had been playing tricks with the mill accounts to such an extent that Martin Doyle had suspected it. When Doyle asked Sir Miles for permission to expand the mill, Sir Miles told him that the profits were so small that this would not be justified. So Doyle asked Sir Miles to let him keep the accounts himself, because he felt that he could prove he was right. He had some significant figures ready to show him when Sir Miles became ill."

"My brother died naturally," said Germaine sharply.

"I think so," said Pat gently, "but Barne—well, there is no need to speculate about what he would have done. Doyle had not got as far as suspecting Barne of stealing money from the mill, but he knew that it was Barne who had destroyed his reputation with Sir Miles, and he refused to speak to him. Barne had a grievance against Doyle for cutting down his revenue by some hundreds of pounds a year. It was Doyle's unconsciousness that saved him from the same fate as Reid.

"I had a long conversation with Miles this afternoon. As soon as he had told me all that he knew I felt safe in trying to trap Barne. He had been very silent and careful. He had not been to Dangan for days before Reid's death, but they had met in Dublin and had had hot discussions about Dangan. There was no need for Barne to conceal the fact that they had met. Reid was supposed to be his friend. I wondered why he had been so secretive, and I came to the conclusion that it was because he had been in Reid's company very recently indeed.

"Reid had written to Barne saying that he was going to approach Martin Doyle and offer him a share in the mill and his rights to Jane Merlin in return for co-operation. Doyle's part was to prove to Miles that the mill should be sold. In fact, Reid said, they could get along very well without Barne. Reid seems to have posted that letter in Dangan early on the day before he died. Later on he wrote to Martin Doyle. He was more worried than he pretended to be about the village agitation against him,

216

not because he cared about the road-house, but because he did not want to be unpopular with people like Paul Walsh and Dr. Donovan. Naturally, the meetings and demonstrations got on his nerves, and he mooned about in a state of indecision for most of the day before his death. He got out his horse that night and rode to Dangan House. When he met Miles he seems to have begun to tell on Barne and then hesitated and stopped, after having given a hint which Miles misinterpreted. Perhaps he was loath to throw away Barne's dubious friendship without giving him another chance.

"However, when Barne called on him the next afternoon he boasted to him that he had already dropped a hint to Miles. Barne had the nicotine—filched some time ago from Dangan House—in a handy little aspirin bottle in his pocket. Reid had poured whisky for both of them in the drawing-room. He was a simple unsuspecting fellow. He went into the next room for the soda-water, and when he came back Barne was innocently sipping his whisky neat. Reid put a shot of soda into his drink and tossed it off, saying that he was going straight over to Dangan House to inform on Barne.

"They left the house together. Barne said that he was going back to Dublin. He had left his car in the avenue and he drove off, simulating fear and anger. Reid marched triumphantly across the park. He must have felt ill on the way, for he seems to have let himself into the house and gone into the study unseen. Later Barne drove innocently up to the door, taking the chance that the nicotine would have overcome Reid on the way across the park. He was delighted to be received like a long-lost friend by Miles.

"Miles never adverted to the fact that Barne could not have had his letter, for it had been posted too late the night before."

"Wasn't it strange that Reid did not call for help when he was dying?" said Germaine.

"Mental confusion is a characteristic symptom of nicotine poisoning, if you remember," said Pat. "I owe you an apology

217

for describing the symptoms at the dinner-table. I wanted to shake Barne into showing some sign of guilt, and get the whole thing over."

"It certainly worked," said Miles. "He's a strange little man. He told me that he was going to make himself believe that Reid was killed in a motor accident. I think he would have been able to do it, too."

There was a little silence which Pat broke by saying:

"Does anyone know Mrs. Barne?"

"I met her once or twice," said Germaine. "I could never make out what bond there could have been between them. She always looked so frightened."

"It's easy to see why," said Pat dryly. "Wives of murderers usually know quite well what's afoot."

Miles described the picture of the skull that Mrs. Barne had hung in Barne's office.

"She obviously knew what she was at, poor woman," he said with a sigh.

"The best thing you can do is to forget about it all——" Pat was saying when suddenly the door burst open. It crashed back so hard that Miles heard the wood splinter around the hinges.

Martin Doyle stood on the threshold, glaring at them. Behind him in the lighted hall they could see Jane Merlin standing listlessly, hardly seeming to notice what was happening. Germaine stood up hurriedly and said:

"Mr. Doyle, Jane should be in bed. She's not fit to go out."

"She's going to the hotel," said Doyle harshly. "I'm sick of this whole place. We're getting out of Dangan in the morning and I hope to God I never lay eyes on any of you again."

"What about your pig-food?" asked Miles, who had not moved.

"To hell with my pig-food!" shouted Doyle. "And to hell with every pig in Ireland!"

"Including the two down at the mill?"

"Them first!" said Doyle recklessly.

He stopped, and a slow grin came in spite of himself. Miles chuckled quietly.

"That's the proper attitude to pigs, in my opinion," he said. He heaved himself out of his chair. "Do come in and sit down. Germaine, will you help Jane back to bed. Or will you stay and have some black coffee, Jane? I've heard that that's the cure."

"I'll stay," she said wearily, and moved past Martin Doyle into the room. "I want to hear all about Mr. Barne and Mr. Reid."

Doyle came slowly across and sat beside her on the sofa. Miles said firmly, emphasizing his words with several jabs at the bell-push with his thumb:

"Inspector Henley will tell you about it to-morrow. I don't want to hear the name of either of those gentlemen again."

Almost before he had finished speaking, James MacDonagh came pounding through the hall. He stood, panting, in the still-open doorway.

"What's up, Sir? What's after happening? Is someone hurted?"

He looked eagerly about the room for the body.

"Could we have a large pot of coffee?" said Miles. "I'm afraid I got carried away."

James looked palpably disappointed, but he shut the door with a resigned air and went off to get the coffee.

"James will find life dull now," said Miles. "We'll all feel the anticlimax. I wonder what we'll do to-morrow?"

"I'll go fishing," said Pat. "I'll have to go down to the hotel for my rod, so perhaps I'll take Paul Walsh with me."

"And take James, of your charity, to carry the bag," said Miles. "What will you do, Germaine?"

"I don't know. I should like to go to Dublin and buy a new dress, but since I don't need a new dress I shouldn't enjoy it at all."

Miles sat up excitedly.

"We'll go to Dublin together," he said eagerly. "We'll visit Mrs. Henley. We'll make her come down to Dangan. We'll have a party. Pat, when did your mother last have a holiday?"

"I don't think she understands the meaning of the word," said Pat with a grin. "I'll bet you five pounds you won't get her to come to Dangan."

"And I'll bet you the same that I will. When I tell her why I want her she won't have the heart to refuse."

"Why do you want her?"

"To change the air of this house," said Miles. "To get rid of the ghosts of Reid and Barne and Merlin—sorry, Jane! I forgot you were here."

"It's all right." She smiled dimly. "Do you think she could get the ghosts out of my house too?"

"You can let them have your house," said Martin Doyle. "You're not going to live there any more."